AFTERMATH
OF DEFIANCE
VOLUME TWO OF THE MAGICAL BOND SERIES

AFTERMATH
OF DEFIANCE
VOLUME TWO OF THE MAGICAL BOND SERIES

A novel
by
A.M. Bochnak

Misadventure Press, Gainesville, Florida, USA

Aftermath of Defiance, Volume Two of the Magical Bond Series

Aftermath of Defiance is a work of fiction. Names, places, characters, and incidents are the product of the author's imagination and are used fictitiously. Any resemblance to actual persons, living or dead, events, or locales is entirely coincidental.

Copyright © 2019 by A.M. Bochnak

Written by A.M. Bochnak

www.ambochnak.com

author@ambochnak.com

All rights reserved.

No part of this publication may be reproduced, distributed or transmitted in any form or by any means, including photocopying, recording, or any other electronic or mechanical methods, without prior written permission of the publisher, except by a reviewer who may quote brief passages in a review.

Published in the United States by Misadventure Press, Gainesville, FL.

www.misadventurepress.com

info@misadventurepress.com

Cover Design by Designs by Angelique

Image Source: Depositphotos

Limits of Liability and Disclaimer Warranty

The author shall not be liable for your misuse of this material. This book is strictly for entertainment purposes.

FIRST EDITION

ISBN (paperback): 978-1-948169-16-5

ISBN (hardcover): 978-1-948169-15-8

ISBN (eBook): 978-1-948169-17-2

ISBN (E4:novella eBook): 978-1-948169-18-9

ISBN (E5:novella eBook): 978-1-948169-19-6

Library of Congress Control Number: 2019905342

Printed in the United States of America

Victoria, Xavier, and Clarice. You are my little rocks. You keep me strong and moving forward daily.

AFTERMATH
OF DEFIANCE
VOLUME TWO OF THE MAGICAL BOND SERIES

THE FATE OF THE ORDER

EPISODE FOUR OF AFTERMATH OF DEFIANCE

CHAPTER ONE

2031: Day 66, Thursday

Connor pressed his pillow hard against his ear to block out the pounding on his door. He wasn't ready to face them, any of them—especially Katrina. He let her down in every way possible. Getting them on and off the island safely had been a complete disaster. He lost his best friend, the closest thing to a brother he ever had. He could've gotten them all killed. He almost did.

Their mission had been simple.

Get in, kill the Enhanced, get out.

That's all they had to do. He knew it was more complicated than that. Killing people, no matter how bad they were, was never easy. But he failed on an epic level. He allowed himself to be persuaded by the others to save the Enhanced instead of killing them. If only he stayed true to the plan, refused to let Ness convince him otherwise, then maybe Ness would still be alive.

He sat up sharply in bed and threw his pillow at the door,

"Go away," he yelled.

"Connor, please," Katrina said, her voice barely audible. "You haven't been out in two days."

A sting of guilt shot through him from the worry he heard in her voice. He hated that worried sound, mostly because he was the reason for it. He was the reason Katrina was no longer cheerful. She had the energy that kept everyone together. The mission, whatever Dr. Hunter had done to her, zapped her energy and made her wary. But nothing took away her compassion. That woman was full of compassion he didn't deserve.

He wrapped his hand around the doorknob and hesitated. Facing her was not something he was ready to do. He needed more time to work through the events that led him to this moment. Stepping back, he sat at the edge of his bed, his body weak, not only from hunger, but from the torture he endured. He had underestimated the strength of Dr. Hunter's magic, a mistake that cost him two lives already.

The deep gashes on his back ached. SUM security had beat him hard, lashed him with a whip. Had it not been for his magical ability, an infection would've weakened him further. Charlotte stood outside his door for hours yesterday begging him to let her heal his wounds, but he refused. He didn't deserve to be let off the hook. He wanted to remember every second of this pain—for Ness and Lina. Even for Maggy, though he never knew her. He was responsible for it, responsible for every event that unfolded, and it was his duty to suffer through it.

Ebony Hunter haunted his thoughts. Horrible images floated in and out of his mind of all the possible things Dr. Hunter could do to her. Every time he closed his eyes he saw her black, dead eyes staring back at him, her body strapped to a gurney, her chest cut open with tubes running in all directions. He would shake that image out of his mind only to have it replaced with rows and rows of large glass jars filled with the hearts of innocent Magical Bond, the heart of Ebony Hunter encased in glass forever.

Surely Dr. Hunter wouldn't dissect his own daughter for magic. *Please, God please don't let that be her fate.* Seeing those bodies of innocent Magical Bond cut open and experimented on was an image that would never leave him. He knew that's where they all would've ended up had she not saved their lives. Ebony was the reason they escaped, the only reason they made it out safely. She sacrificed herself for them, strangers she hardly knew. And what had he done? Nothing. He didn't have the strength or courage to save his best friend.

The black and white checkered tiles on the floor blended together as his vision blurred. The tears he kept bottled up inside ever since Ness' death finally escaped. Everything happened so fast at the end, he never had time to mourn his friend. Losing Ebony on top of Ness' loss was more than he could process. He no longer contained his emotions. His head dropped into his hands, and Connor sobbed for the first time since he was a young child.

Ebony was not a part of his plan, nor were these feelings she invoked. She had mesmerized him. How, he had no idea, but she had done it nonetheless. From the first moment he laid eyes on her, he knew there was something special about her.

He gave in to his emotions and his body trembled under his tears. The more his body shook, the deeper his wounds cut. Tears ran down his face and blood ran down his back. He had to find the strength to pull himself up and fight back. He had to find a way to forgive himself.

Ebony was still alive. She had to be. Her father wouldn't have killed her right away.

He hoped.

Even if she was dead, he had to fight to stop Dr. Hunter and all of SUM from playing God. *Like they had some divine right to fuck with our genetic code.*

He fell onto his bed, ignoring the pain that shot down his back and all the way to his toes. It didn't help that his bed was hard as rocks. He couldn't deny the other side lived in luxury. Even the test subjects destined for the chopping block were given rooms better than anything he'd ever seen out here. Unlike the large, bright room with a beautiful view of the city he was given in the Institute, his room at headquarters was tiny and dark. All the living quarters were underground in what once functioned as a parking lot back when everyone could afford cars. The rooms were partitioned with thin walls made of scrap metal and concrete blocks worked together like a three-dimensional puzzle creating small, personal spaces for each member. Not every room had a door that locked like Connor's. There were a few privileges for being the leader. But that was sure to end soon. He'd lose them all as soon as the council voted him out.

The loud pounding started up again. This time it was Sullivan who called out his name. "Connor, come on man. Either open this door or we're gonna break it down."

"I said, go away," he yelled. He knew what they wanted, and he didn't care. All he wanted was to be left alone for a few days. He would deal with them and the others later.

"Connor!" Katrina's voice was louder this time. "You have to let us in. Marc is gathering support for a special council meeting. You know what that means."

"Fuck," Connor said under his breath. That asshole couldn't wait, could he? He'd been dying for a reason to get rid of him and now he had his chance.

"Connor!" She pounded again. "This doesn't look good for you. The other members are talking, questioning your ability. They think you're no longer fit to lead. You have to come out and show them Marc is wrong."

"It doesn't matter." He'd never find peace, never rest. If his mind didn't torment him, his friends would. He let out a deep sigh, got up and opened the door. He stared at the others.

Katrina ran into the room and wrapped her arms around him. He tensed under her touch and pulled her arms away from his back.

"Sorry," she said.

"It's okay." He turned towards to his bed, the back of his shirt streaked in blood, and sat down. "Marc is going to do what Marc wants no matter what any of us say."

"True, but you still have to fight for what's right. We all do." Katrina sat down next to him. Sullivan leaned on the opposite wall of his bed and Charlotte shut the door. The gang was together again, at least what was left of them.

"I screwed up, it's over."

"No, it's not. We still have a fight to win."

"There is no we." He shifted over, creating more space between him and Katrina. "I failed. I got people killed."

"Oh, shut up and stop whinin'," Sullivan yelled from across the room. "Yes, we lost some friends on both sides. It sucks. That's what happens in war."

"I'm not whining, asshole." Connor shot a look in Sullivan's direction. "Don't you get it? None of it mattered."

"Yeah, I get it. More than you could ever imagine." Sullivan stepped close to Connor and glared down at him. "In case you weren't listenin', the parents Char and I mourned, the ones who were killed right in front of us, weren't our parents. And let's not forget, for the last month Dr. Hunter's been messin' with my mind. Literally. Process that, asshole."

"Get out of my face." Connor stood and pushed Sullivan back. "I'm not trying to be insensitive, but this is over. Get it? There's nothing we can do when SUM is playing so unfair."

"This isn't about fairness." Sullivan stiffened, visibly fighting the urge to lunge towards Connor. "Nothin' in life is fair. Why the hell would you even expect them to play fair? That's gotta be the dumbest thing you've ever said."

"Calm down, Sully." Katrina touched his arm. "This isn't helping."

"Like I give a shit if I help him."

"Enough!" Charlotte glared at her bother before she walked over and laid her hands on Connor's shoulders. "This is stupid. You're both being stupid."

"No!" Connor knocked her hand off him. He refused to let her heal him. Suffering through this was his choice.

"I don't care if you get mad at me." Charlotte wrapped her fingers tight around his wrist and pulled him close. "I don't care if you ever speak to me again. I'm doing this."

He struggled to free himself, but Katrina stepped behind him and pressed close to keep him from pulling away. A glow radiated from Charlotte's hand where she held his wrist as she healed him. He attempted to wiggle free, but in his weakened state, he was no match for them. Crying out, he begged them to stop, but they didn't listen. If he hadn't already felt worthless, being sandwiched between them, unable to fight them off, completely crushed him. Sullivan leaned against the opposite wall and watched the girls take Connor down. They pinned him down on the bed, and Charlotte's magic worked its way up his arm, then down his back. He let out a muffled cry as her power stitched up his back, each cut pulled back together. The skin bonded together to become one again and the healing process took less than a minute.

Connor pushed Katrina and Charlotte off him with ease

once his wounds were healed. Charlotte's magic even took away his aching hunger. "Just leave me alone."

"It had to be done, Connor." Katrina rested her hand on his back.

He jerked his body forward, causing her hand to fall.

"We need you," Katrina said.

"She's right," Charlotte said. "It doesn't matter what the council does, they have no idea what we're up against. We have to continue what you started. If we back down now, there's no telling what SUM might do next."

"We don't have a choice," Sullivan said. He stood in front of Connor, a somber look in his eyes. "None of us. We have to keep fightin', together. This will never end until one of us wins. We can't let SUM win."

"No," Connor said. "The last thing I need right now is a verbal beat down from Marc."

"Get over it." Sullivan grabbed him by the arms and forced Connor to look at him. "It's not about what you need. This is about all of us. This is about everyone out there sufferin'."

"Get off my case, Sully." Connor pushed him up against the wall, his anger heightened. Connor wanted to hit something, someone, anyone. He didn't care if Sullivan deserved it not. But he resisted the urge to punch him in the face. He shouldn't be mad at them, they were only trying to help. Connor was too unstable to contain his actions and he was taking it out on the wrong people. He let go of Sullivan and stepped back. "Go without me. I give you permission to speak on my behalf."

"Stop right now!" Katrina yelled so loud the walls shook like a rolling wave of thunder came crashing through the room. Sparks of flame shot out of her fingertips and her eyes glowed an orange-red hue. "You're still our leader. Act like it." She spoke with authority, her voice harsh and demanding.

Connor's face went blank. In all the years he'd known her, she never lost her temper. She was always the calm, reasonable one. But with the burning look in her eyes, all reason was gone. He could see her frustration rise as her body began to glow a deep orange and her hair turned into bright red flames.

"I'm sorry, Kat." His head hung low and his shoulders dropped.

He had no fight left in him, not even to fight off his friends from doing what was right. The words they spoke rang true, and he would step up and do the right thing when the time came. He always did, no matter how hard he resisted. He'd hoped it would wait a few days longer, but his hope was crushed. "Do whatever has to be done. I'll be there."

"You're not the only one who lost someone they loved, Connor. You would do well to remember that." Katrina opened the door to leave but turned to Connor before walking out. "I'm going to try my best to delay this meeting, but you better get it together fast. There may be no stopping Marc."

CHAPTER TWO

2031: Day 66, Thursday

Katrina's head ached from losing her temper with Connor. Her power had never quite manifested itself like that before and it invoked unwanted feelings. Her magic, the power that swelled inside her, was fighting to escape. She was dangerously close to losing control of it and had she not left, her power would've unleashed itself. She had always viewed her magic as her protector, but just now, whatever happened when she yelled at Connor, it felt more like a weapon. She felt disjointed ever since the day Dr. Hunter violated her by pulling her magic out of her against her will. Her bond with her magic, her intuition and ability to communicate with it, had been disrupted.

She forced herself to take slow, steady breaths—a form of walking meditation—to draw her magic back in. She was failing and with every step she took, her magic strengthened and resisted her tug. It wanted to be free, to rage against the enemy, but the enemy was not here.

It didn't help that her scalp tingled from an intense heat that she swore was burning her hair from her head. But there were no flames, no blisters. Only a soft red glow down at the tips of her hair. The ends of her hair, each perfectly formed curl, radiated a heat that could burn this place down. She ran her fingers through it in the hopes of making it go away. She was certain it would burn her hands, but when she touched her hair, all she felt was hair and heat. The red glow of energy transferred to her fingers and the glow spread through her hand, then up her arm. It didn't make any sense. How could she possibly feel the heat radiating from all around her and not get burned?

Her emotions were in a whirlwind, spiraling into a place she did not recognize. She lost control of her emotions after Dr. Hunter altered her magic. It was his magic that pulled on hers and forced it to show its full strength, not her doing.

The intense heat and fire was a power she did not know she possessed.

So much had happened to her, to all of them, over the past few weeks. It's no wonder her magic was a little on the fritz. Connor's current state of whining only made it worse. She'd seen him deal with some serious stuff in the past and he'd never lost it like this before. She didn't want to seem insensitive, losing Ness and Lina was difficult for all of them, but he was their leader. He'd lost people before and never fell apart like this. He had a reputation to maintain, a certain level of expectation he couldn't fall below. He had better pull it together and fast. If what she heard about Marc was true, they had another battle on the horizon.

She had to convince Marc to delay the council meeting. Putting Connor in front of them when he was like this would not end well.

She set out to find him, but Marc was either hiding from her or had found a new place to hang out. His room was empty—so were the lounge and kitchen. Someone was always in the lounge watching television, but not today. Every place she checked she was met with silence. Fear took over her thoughts as she began to imagine the worst. Marc was up to something and whatever it was, it wasn't good.

She'd walked all over headquarters searching for Marc and found nothing. The walking, at least, was a distraction and her magic relaxed. She felt like herself once again. No more glowing red hair or radiating heat from her body. She stopped by the kitchen and poured herself a glass of water.

There it was.

A small sign was posted on the communication board. Marc was recruiting troops to join his cause, whatever it was, and they were in the recreation center across the street.

THAT BASTARD. EXPANDING AND CREATING the rec center had been one of Connor's first initiatives as the new Order leader. Marc had been against it from the beginning and fought Connor tooth and nail when the council voted to expand to the building across the street. It was too dangerous, Marc said. He was so sure if they expanded and created a safe place for Order members to exercise, and "play," as he put it, they would jeopardize the location of headquarters. Marc had been wrong, of course, but to choose this location for his grand attempt to take out Connor was low.

The moment she stepped inside the rec center, the location of the crowd was easily recognized by the low rumble that filled the entrance. At least Marc was smart enough to lead them underground and hold this rally in the main courts in the basement. With as much noise as they made, anywhere on the first floor would've drawn a crowd from outside.

Nearly every member that lived at headquarters was

present. Some stood in silence, but most were yelling and cheering Marc on like he was their messiah. From the back of the room, she couldn't make out a word Marc was saying. The noise from the crowd was too loud.

Slowly, she began pushing her way through. Some stepped out of her way and let her pass, but others were aggressive and blocked her path, refusing to let her pass. Despite the obstacles, she pushed forward.

By the time she made it halfway through the crowd, her temper flared. This time she was in complete control of her magic. She would not let Marc's scheming get the best of her.

So many people were packed into this small space. She never would've imagined so many could fit. What had gotten into these people? She wasn't exactly friends with any of them, but some of them were good acquaintances. Jenny, for example. Katrina had drunk plenty of beers with her. They joked and shared childhood stories often. Today, though, Jenny spat in her face and called her a traitor. Katrina clenched her fists and fought the urge to hit Jenny in the face with a fireball. The way these people were acting, it was as if none of them remembered her.

Tired of getting smacked around, she centered her energy and called upon her power over air. A slight breeze pulled down from the ceiling and circled her body in the form of a weak wind tunnel. As her power strengthened so did the force of the wind. The people closest to her rushed upon the others around them, creating a hole in the crowd where Katrina stood. She had not called upon her power of fire, but her hair started to glow in red flames as the wind blew it back behind her. She forced a gust of wind through the middle of the crowd that blocked her view of Marc. Bodies were thrown to the side in piles, opening a clear path to him.

The room fell silent.

"Well, well, well." A devilish grin covered Marc's face. He stepped down from his makeshift platform and walked towards Katrina with slow, steady steps. "It's Connor's lap dog here to deal with his problems for him."

"Don't be a fool, Marc." The flames of her hair grew and the wind tunnel around her pulled back towards her, concentrating around her body. "You need to stop feeding this mob lies. You have no clue what we're up against."

"Lies?" He threw his head back as he let out a deep, menacing laugh. "Just another ploy for power. The only threat we have to worry about is Connor and SUMs spies that you guys led right to our secret headquarters. All of our lives are at risk now."

"You don't know what you're talking about." She released some of her hold on the air and the wind tunnel around her began to dissipate. "SUM is much more dangerous than we realized. We must ban together. We have to—"

"How can we trust anything you say?" Marc stopped close to her face and stared into her eyes, daring her to continue. He turned to the crowd, his arms stretched out to his side. "Katrina and Connor defied a council ruling, a ruling we voted down out of fear of losing lives."

A cheer of rage filled the crowd. Katrina didn't just hear the rage, she felt it. He looked back at Katrina, his face hard, and pointed a finger at her. "They betrayed us all. Traitors. As a result, two innocent Order members were killed. We cannot afford to listen to their lies any longer."

The mob around them cheered at Marc's words. For someone with no magical abilities, he had a strong hold on this crowd. He must've been promoting his cause from the moment they left. Maybe they had been stupid for leaving and executing the mission without the vote. But they learned so much—things that would help them end this war between the

Magical Bond and the Common Blood.

"Marc, please." She let go of her magic and it retreated deep within her. "You have to stop this."

"I will not stop until you, Connor, and those spies are gone." The mob cheered again.

Katrina's shoulders dropped. With every cheer from the crowd, she felt more defeated. How could it have gotten this bad while they were gone? She focused her stare on his face, fighting to hold back the sadness threatening to replace her anger. "Then our end is near."

"If that's the case," Marc said, squaring his stance. "Then you and Connor are to blame."

CHAPTER THREE

2031: Day 67, Friday

Connor squinted, shielding his eyes when the fluorescent lights above flickered on. His early morning alone time was over. He'd been sitting in the dark, drinking his coffee, for over an hour, hoping to remain undisturbed for a bit longer. Checking the clock on the wall, it was 4:52 a.m. He expected to sit in peace until after six, but someone else must have had the same idea.

He debated ducking out the side door and avoiding whoever was coming this way. He had thirty seconds to make his escape before whoever turned the lights on arrived at the kitchen. The controls to the kitchen lights were located down the hall at the main entrance to the community room—one of the many downfalls to converting an underground parking garage into a living space. There was limited electrical outlets and wiring.

Connor stayed where he was, drinking his coffee. With any luck, it'd be someone that didn't know him and would be too afraid to stick around long.

"He lives," Sullivan mumbled under a yawn. He hadn't even bothered to get dressed and was still in his boxer briefs and t-shirt. It was his slippers that caught Connor's attention: fuzzy pink bunnies with big floppy ears. *Where did he find those?*

"You're up early." Connor filled his mug up with fresh coffee and headed for the door. After the way Sullivan acted yesterday, he was in no hurry to be alone in a room with him. Connor still felt the urge to punch him in the face. With his emotional state in turmoil, he had trouble letting yesterday go.

"Don't leave on my account." Sullivan pulled a tray of leftover macaroni and cheese out of the refrigerator and grabbed a fork before he sat down. "Stay."

"No thank you." Connor paused in the doorway. "I've no interest in listening to your shit again today."

"Well." Sullivan looked up at him and smiled. Connor paused, caught off guard by the mischievous look in his eyes. It was the same look he'd seen in Sullivan's eyes weeks ago when he first met him in the institution. "So long as you're done with all that whinin' there won't be shit to go on about."

Connor watched him for a moment, shoveling food into his mouth like nothing else mattered except eating. Considering their situation and the current state of the world, it seemed wrong. Then again what else could they do at this hour? Might as well enjoy what small moments of peace they could get. This was probably going to be a mistake, but Connor grabbed a fork and joined him. He skipped dinner last night to avoid conflict and that macaroni and cheese looked good, even if it was cold.

They ate in silence, neither bothered to look at the other.

Feeling full, Connor put his fork down and watched Sullivan continue to stuff food in his mouth. He couldn't imagine where Sullivan put it all. He'd eaten through half the dish on his own.

Tired from lack of sleep and exhausted from all the drama, Connor needed to put their troubles behind him. He wasn't ready to do it, but he needed to do it. That was the only way he'd be able to move on, find a way to save Ebony, and end this war against SUM. But before he could do that, he had to face the council. Making amends with Sullivan before the meeting would help him clear his mind and calm his anger.

"Look, Sully, sorry about yesterday," he said.

"Don't sweat it." Sullivan didn't even look up. He was too focused on eating and showed no sign of caring that they fought yesterday.

Connor chuckled. "Yeah, okay." He stood to get more coffee, one more cup and then he'd have to cut himself off. With the day he was in for, he was going to need extra energy, but not at the expense of his magic. "Want any coffee?"

"Coffee would be great. Thanks." Sullivan pushed the tray aside and slouched back in his chair. He was finally full. "You ready for that council meetin' today?"

"Does a dog fly?" Connor handed Sullivan the mug and sat down.

"I guess not." Sullivan laughed. "So where do we go when they kick you guys out? I mean, Char and I are not exactly welcomed here. I thought these guys were your friends."

"We may not get kicked out," Connor said, hopeful.

"Dude, who you kiddin'?" Sullivan dropped his laugh. "They're kickin' you out."

"Maybe so, but I'm going to do my best to fight it." He leaned his head back and stared at the ceiling, doing his best to avoid the glare from the fluorescent lighting. Katrina had stopped by last night and told him what she witnessed with the mob. Marc didn't waste any time building an army against him. He must have started gathering followers the moment they left. While Marc's behavior disturbed him, it was the other council members that he was most concerned about. Katrina said they'd lost them all. Even Elle, who'd always supported him regardless of the circumstances, had turned against him. As much as he hated to admit it, Sullivan was probably right. "And if they do, we have places to go where I have friends that'd be glad to have our help."

"Good," Sullivan said. "Cause Char and I are ready to get out of this place."

CONNOR TURNED THE LAST CORNER down the hall leading to the conference room and bumped into Katrina. He hadn't expected her to be waiting at the edge of the hall and almost knocked her to the ground.

"Sorry about that." He gave her a gentle smile and squeezed her hand. At least he could still count on Katrina's support no matter the mistakes he made. Having her by his side today meant more to him than he could express with words. If he couldn't convince the council to let them stay, to continue the fight against SUM, then he was going to lose one of the only good things he ever had in his life. The Order gave him a purpose he truly believed in and was willing to die for.

"You ready?" Katrina asked.

"As ready as anyone can be." He nodded and headed down the hall. No use delaying this meeting any longer. Any hope he had been holding onto, Sullivan squashed earlier this morning with his blunt honesty. Connor created this situation when he defied the council's ruling. He'd do his best to argue his case, to convince them not to kick him and Katrina off the council, but if the table was turned and it was one of them, he'd vote to kick them out. No doubt about it.

He stopped just outside the door and listened to the sound of the voices inside. They were arguing, or at least Marc was yelling. The yelling stopped, and the room fell silent the second Connor and Katrina stepped through the door. He looked at each member. Nola looked bored—she picked at her nails and ignored everyone. Elle and Silka dropped their heads, avoiding eye contact, and Marc fixed his eyes on Connor, then smiled.

"Good of you to join us today, Connor," Marc said. "I'm glad we can get this done now. Looks like I lose the bet."

"What bet is that?" Connor held his gaze, his lips pinched tight.

"I didn't think you'd bother to show up today. The ladies insisted you would. I bet them my dessert tonight and I lost." He let out a low laugh.

"You seem to have made a remarkable recovery." Elle spoke up before Marc dominated the conversation with his useless diversion. Connor shifted his gaze in her direction. She avoided making eye contact with him. She pretended to write something on the paper in front of her instead of looking at him. "You were in pretty bad shape when you arrived."

"Charlotte healed me." He took a few steps in her direction. A tinge of pain settled in his stomach. Elle had always been one of his biggest supporters and allies. Had his decision to disobey a council ruling been that bad? He knew the consequences of his decision would be harsh, but he never expected to lose Elle's support. He considered using his power over her mind to force her to look at him but decided against it. Using his power on her wouldn't win her back to his side.

"What do you mean?" She set her pen down and looked around the room, still avoiding his stare. "How did she heal you?"

"She possesses the power of healing. She can heal wounds and bring the recently deceased back to life."

"How is that possible?" Elle asked. She shook her head, blocking Connor's view of her face, but Connor saw the look of surprise in her eyes before she hid it.

"Her magical abilities were enhanced by SUM." Connor pushed his shoulders back and crossed his arms over his chest. He wasn't looking forward to this conversation, but he had to tell them the truth. They needed to know what they were up against with SUM—who they really were. "We all were. Well, Sullivan, Katrina, and I, that is."

"What do you mean by enhanced?" Elle turned back to her notebook and started writing again. Her facial expression didn't fluctuate or show any sign she understood what he just said.

"SUM manipulated our magical genes during fetal development." Connor deliberately spoke in a matter-of-fact tone. The anger inside him grew at her lack of response and he needed her, all of them, to understand what SUM had done. He had to keep his emotions in check, stay calm. "As a result, we have enhanced superpowers."

"You mean to tell me," Marc cut in, "You, Kat, and those other two were manipulated as a fetus?"

"Yes." Connor sighed and shifted in Marc's direction. "Our entire lives were planned out for us by SUM. Nothing happened by chance."

"This is absurd." Marc adjusted in his seat. At least he was responding to the news Connor was breaking to them. That was more than he could say for the others. "Did they brainwash you while you were there, too?"

"I get that this sounds crazy." Katrina leaned on the table

towards Marc and stared him dead in the eyes. "SUM has been playing us all along. Our lives, our decisions, were never ours. SUM very carefully orchestrated every step we've ever taken. Nothing happened to us by chance."

"How is that possible?" Silka stood. Her hands shook despite her attempt at hiding them behind her back. "Is that also true for us?"

"No, it's only us," Connor answered. "At least that we know of. SUM is much more powerful than we anticipated. The extent they are willing to go to ensure their cause is successful is limitless. They don't care whose life is lost, or how many for that matter."

"But." Elle shook her head. Her face said it all. She didn't believe a word he was saying. Either he misread her brief moment of surprise earlier or it hadn't been there. "Why you guys?"

"Why not?" Connor tossed the question out to the group. If he didn't convince them soon, he never would. Marc wouldn't hold back much longer before he turned the conversation towards Connor's future in the Order. He had one shot at this. Once they kicked him off the council, he'd never get the chance to address them again. "How else do you explain our advanced magical ability, advanced beyond anything any Magical Bond in history has ever been able to do? It actually makes a lot of sense when you think about it. It wasn't merely by chance we all happened to be born around the same time with powers unlike anything ever seen before. It was by design. SUM's design."

"So, you were planted here by SUM?" Marc said, folding his arms across his chest.

"No, we weren't planted." Connor kept his voice calm. He refused to let Marc get under his skin.

"How do we know that?" Marc slammed his fist on the

table.

"We weren't," Connor whispered. He dropped his head, feeling the weight of the world on his shoulders once again. He knew this would be hard for them to believe. He knew it would be impossible to convince Marc, but he had to find a way to get through to the others. He lifted his head and took a deep breath before continuing. "We were placed in various home environments, exposed to different emotional stressors to see how our magical abilities would develop as a result of those emotions."

"That doesn't make any sense." Elle looked confused. "Why all this trouble?"

"Because magic is dying. The Magical Bond is in danger of extinction, at least that's how Dr. Hunter sees it."

"He thinks we're losing magic?" Silka asked.

"No, not exactly." Connor saw fear in Silka's eyes while Elle and Marc maintained their looks of disbelief. If he could win Silka over, there was hope. "How do I say this? He thinks this is an evolutionary flaw that is preferentially creating a weaker, new species of humans. The Common Blood."

"But we're all one species?" Marc said.

"I didn't say I believed this. That's not how Dr. Hunter sees it. He thinks of the Magical Bond and Common Blood as two separate species. The Magical Bond is threatened by extinction unless he makes them stronger and weeds out the Common Blood."

"That's the dumbest thing I've ever heard." Marc let out a nervous laugh. "We're not that different from each other, not really."

Connor glanced at Elle, who he could see was thinking about what he said. Her expression softened. "I'm only telling you what he said. He's trying to strengthen the Magical Bond and find a way to give the Common Blood magic. He's using us to try to do that. If his restoration attempts fail, he will kill all Common Blood."

The room fell silent. Connor could sense their anger and doubt weaken as they contemplated his words. He turned towards Katrina and she smiled with a reassuring nod. *Am I getting through to them?* That seemed like too much to hope for and a little too easy if that was the case. Marc especially. He expected a fight from him, but he hardly raised his voice. Marc's calmness worried him more than if he'd yelled and threatened. It was out of character. And if the size of the mob Marc gathered was as large as Katrina said it was, he had no intention of giving into him. Still, this brief moment of contemplation gave him hope and a little bit of strength.

"Why emotions?" Marc's face hardened again, and Connor felt every bit of his anger return.

"Magic is tied to our emotions," Connor said, calmly. "The better control we have of our emotions, the better control we have over our magic. Control and Magic go hand in hand."

"I find all this hard to believe," Marc huffed. He looked to Elle and Silka for agreement, but they stared at the empty space in front of them and didn't notice his glance. "And this Dr. Hunter character, he told you his plan."

"Not at first." Connor shrugged. "But yeah, he answered every question I asked him."

"Why would he do that?" Elle asked. Her expression of disbelief remained, but Connor sensed her internal struggle. Her mind opened up a little to the words he said.

"He didn't think we would ever leave the island again. He assumed he had us right where he wanted us and where he needed us. He's a very arrogant man."

"You do realize how ridiculous this all sounds?" Elle said.

"If you met Dr. Hunter, it wouldn't seem so ridiculous." Connor had to agree with her there. This all sounded farfetched. Aside from bringing Sullivan and Charlotte in to tell them their side of things, which was a bad idea considering how the Order felt about them, he wasn't sure how else to convince them he was telling them the truth. "Look, we could talk about this all day long, but this is not the issue."

"We're going to talk about this," Marc demanded. "We need to know the truth, not some wild story about your adventures with SUM."

"We need to stop SUM." Connor raised his voice for the first time since entering the room. Katrina slipped her hand on his arm and sent him a rush calmness with her magic. He cracked his neck and refocused. "SUM is planning destruction for all Common Blood. Marc, you of all people should want to stop that. Talking about it will not stop SUM."

"Stopping SUM, yes. But trusting you, after all you did? I don't think so." Marc stood and squared his shoulders towards Connor, his chest puffed out.

"You can trust me, Marc." Connor held strong in his position and refused to let his body flinch. "I'm still the same guy."

"You're one of them. You just said as much." Marc poked Connor in the chest, but Connor was ready for it and his body didn't move an inch. He sensed Marc's intentions before he made a move.

"No, that's not what I said." Connor inched forward, his nose close to Marc's. He was losing Marc, and his temper flared. Not a good combination.

"You just told us you were made by SUM. How is that not one of them?" Marc took a step back.

Connor sensed fear taking hold of Marc's emotions, but he tried hard to fight it and stay focused on anger. "Just because—"

"Stop," Elle interjected. "Let's all take a step back. We have other items to discuss before we can make any decisions about SUM."

"Yes." Marc let himself fall back into his chair. "Yes, we do."

"Connor, Katrina, please sit." Elle pointed to the two chairs on the opposite end of the table.

"Nothing else matters." Connor glared at her and threw his hands up in the air. He lost control of the conversation fast. He needed more time to convince them he was telling them the truth.

"Sit down, Connor." Elle raised her voice, daring Connor to object further. Katrina pulled a chair out and sat down, then motioned for Connor to do the same.

"Connor Vance," Elle said as she pulled two pieces of paper out from underneath her folder, "you are charged with a direct violation against this council. You knowingly disregarded the final decision of this council. You organized and carried out an unapproved mission. You are hereby stripped of your title of Leader of the Order of Peace, removed from your council seat, and banned from the Order of Peace indefinitely."

"What!" Connor gasped. He expected to lose his title and be removed from the council, but he never imagined they would ban him from the Order altogether. They needed him and his magic. "Isn't that taking this a little too far?"

"You got two members killed," Marc yelled.

"Enough!" Elle shot her hand in Marc's direction, demanding silence. "Katrina Hicks, you are charged with a direct violation against this council. You knowingly disregarded the final decision of this council and helped carry out an unapproved mission. You are hereby removed from your council seat and banned from the Order of Peace indefinitely."

Connor stood and looked at each of them. Silka kept her head down, and Nola never said a word. But Elle made direct eye contact with him for the first time since entering this room. Her face was hard and Connor knew her decision was final. Nothing he said would change her mind. He lost this fight and failed at convincing them of SUM's true plans. "You're making a huge mistake. You'll never survive SUM without our help."

"You have one week to vacate the premises. I think you'll find those terms are quite generous. We've even decided to let your friends stay until you leave." Elle slid copies of the council's termination ruling across the table to them. Connor glanced down at his copy, Elle's signature in black ink.

"You can't be serious." Katrina scanned the notice, her hand shaking when she picked it up. "You can't do this. You need us."

"As the interim leader, I can do this. It is done." Elle nodded at Marc and he stood to open the door. Two security guards stepped in and directed Connor and Katrina to leave. "Good day."

"You have no idea what you've just done." Connor walked out, Katrina behind him. He expected to get kicked off the council, but banned from the Order? He never considered that an option. He expected this kind of response from Marc, but not Elle. She had always been reasonable, and supportive even in times of mistakes. Apparently, the days of being reasonable were past them.

CHAPTER FOUR

2031: Day 67, Friday

Despite the speed at which Connor walked back to his room, it felt like the longest walk of his life. All he was and had been for years was stripped away with a single signature. His purpose in life was gone, reduced to nothing more than a common citizen. What did that even mean? He'd never been a common citizen in his life. He'd gone from the orphanage, to homeless, to the Order. The largest chunk of his life had been with the Order.

"Connor, please," Katrina called after him. "Stop. We have to talk about this."

"What's there to talk about?" He didn't want to talk about this. He knew what this meant, and talking about it would only slow them down. They had to get out of there before Marc's mob turned against them and came after Sullivan and Charlotte. He couldn't keep them safe without the support of the council and he no longer had their support. "They made their decision. We need to leave now."

"Let's talk about this first." She caught his arm and pulled him around to face her.

"I'm done talking. Talking gets people killed." Connor brushed her off and entered his room. In anticipation of this outcome, he started packing his bags last night. He pulled the last of his things out of his closet and stuffed it into a bag without folding a thing. Katrina sat down on the bed and dropped her head into her hands.

"Please, Connor." She begged. "Give it a few more days. They gave us a week. We can change their minds."

"Change whose mind?" Sullivan asked from the doorway, Charlotte next to him. They were already packed when they walked into Connor's room. They didn't have much, a small duffel bag each with a few changes of clothing Katrina gathered for them when they first arrived.

"We're leaving today." Connor was focused on one thing—packing.

"That good, uh?" Sullivan stepped into the room and sat down next to Katrina. "What'd they say?"

"They didn't just kick us off the council, they banned us from the Order indefinitely." Katrina rubbed her hands over her eyes before she fell back on the bed and stretched her arms over her head.

"Kat, you need to go pack now." Connor tossed the last of his belongings into the bag and zipped it closed. "We need to get out of here."

"I can't believe this is happening," Katrina said. "And I can't believe you're giving up so quickly, Connor."

"I'm not giving up," he yelled. He couldn't believe he had to explain this to her of all people. She knew how the council worked and once a decision was made, it was final. "Think about it for a moment, from their perspective."

"I don't give a shit about their perspective!" Katrina yelled.

"I didn't say they were right, but I understand why they think what they've done is the right thing to do. We disobeyed a direct order from the council. I would've made the same decision, so would you, if someone else disobeyed a decision the council made."

Connor dropped his head into his hand and rubbed his eyes. Would he have done the same thing? He would've voted them off the council for sure, but he would've taken into consideration the circumstances, the reason for the defiance, and would've never banned them from the Order.

"I get what you're saying, I do." Katrina fought back the tears. She loved the Order. They had become her family, her reason for living. "Concessions have to be made during times of war. They're being unreasonable."

"I'm sorry, Kat." Connor reached out to her, but she pulled away. "There's nothing else I can do. The decision is final."

"And you think leaving is the answer!" Katrina grabbed his bag and threw it at him. It hit his chest with a thud.

"Ouch, why'd you do that?" He scooped up the bag and tossed it back on the bed.

"Connor, what will we do?" Katrina begged. She was angry, and he could feel the pain through her magic. She never thought it would come to this, neither of them did. While he accepted their fate, she assumed they would fix it, find a way to convince the others to let them stay.

"I'm sorry Kat, but..."

"Sully!" Charlotte, who had been standing in the doorway this whole time, ran quickly to her brother. Sullivan had fallen onto the floor. "You okay?"

Charlotte rolled Sullivan onto his back. His face was blank, his eyes wide open. The color left his face and he began to tremble. His legs thrashed and he scratched at his neck.

"Sully, what's wrong?" Charlotte cupped her hands on his face, pulling him forward to look into his eyes.

"It's too late," he whispered.

"What's too late?" Connor asked.

Before Sullivan could answer a thunderous roar echoed through the room and the walls began to shake. A shrill of screams came next, followed by pounding footsteps running down the hall. Connor ran to the door only to see a mass of people running away from rapid gunfire coming from the direction of the main entrance.

"Shit." Connor shut the door. "We're under attack. We gotta go, now."

"It's too late," Sullivan said again, this time louder. He sat up, his color restored. "I led them here."

"What?" Charlotte squeezed his hands. "Who's here?"

"Snap out of it." Connor knocked Charlotte out of the way and pulled Sullivan to his feet. "Whatever this is, it's gonna have to wait. We gotta get out of here."

"SUM. They found me." Sullivan stood frozen, his eyes fixed on the floor.

The sound of the gunfire grew louder. If SUM truly had found them, they were working their way closer to their location. If this was SUM, nothing would ever get Connor or Katrina reinstated into the Order. The Order headquarters had been securely hidden in this location for over twenty years without discovery. If this was SUM, Connor was the one who led them to the Order headquarters.

Connor ran to the picture on the wall and removed it to reveal a hidden compartment. He pulled out a large duffel bag followed by a smaller backpack. Behind the bags were several guns. He grabbed one and opened the duffel bag. It was packed full of ammunition. He pulled out a box and handed it and the gun to Katrina.

"Do you two know how to use a gun?" Connor looked at Charlotte, calm and collected. This he was prepared for. If the day ever came that headquarters was attacked, he made sure he was prepared. He unzipped a side pouch on the bag and flipped through several maps until he found the right one.

"No." Charlotte shook her head. "I've never held one before."

"You stick close to Kat. Sully, you're with me." Connor unfolded the map and pointed to the area that represented his room.

"We only have to make it three doors down. That's our safe route out of here." He pointed the door on the map not far from their current location. Connor stuffed a few more guns in the duffel bag before zipping it closed and tossing it over his shoulder. He tossed the backpack to Katrina. The sound of gunfire was getting closer. "There's a secret passage that will lead us to the subway system."

"We gotta hurry, Connor." Katrina cracked the door open. "The hall is clear, but I hear footsteps running this way."

"Go! Stick close together. We'll see you in the tunnel. Do not stop under any circumstance, understand?" She nodded at him before she grabbed Charlotte and slipped out the door.

"Let's go, Sully. It's now or never." Connor grabbed him and dragged him out the door. They were seconds behind Katrina and Charlotte and the hallway was already full of smoke. The sound of gunfire rang behind them, much closer than mere moments ago. Connor hugged the wall, staying as low as possible. The challenge was Sullivan. He was not fully alert and struggled to stay on his feet. It was either leave him behind or drag him along. Connor wasn't about to leave any of them behind, so he hugged Sullivan close and pulled him along the wall.

Connor was almost to the door when he felt a sharp sting in his arm. He fell to the floor, losing his grip on Sullivan causing them both to crash to the floor. The footsteps of the intruders were behind them, within feet of where they laid. The only thing keeping them safe was the blanket of smoke filling the hall. Connor pushed himself up to his knees. The pain in his arm made him dizzy and he collapsed again.

"Shit! Man, you're hit." Their crash to the floor had, at least momentarily, snapped Sullivan out of his trance.

Connor looked at his arm, his eyes struggled to focus. He was shot in his bicep; the bullet went clean through.

"We've gotta get out of here," Sullivan said.

"The door." Connor blinked his eyes into focus and pointed to the door less than a foot in from of them. Sullivan didn't hesitate. He grabbed hold of Connor and dragged him to the door offering them a way out. Voices yelled behind them—so close they could grab them if they could see them. Staying low to the ground, Sullivan opened the door and pushed Connor through.

"Lock the door," Connor yelled after Sullivan dropped him on the ground. "Hurry. The... grate... open the grate." Connor pointed to the grate on the floor in the corner.

Sullivan ignored him and inspected his arm. The bullet went straight through and he was losing a lot of blood. Sullivan pulled his shirt off and tied it tight around his arm. The intruders were right outside the door firing rounds in attempts to break through.

"We have... have to go," Connor said. His head spun, and he struggled to focus his eyes on Sullivan, but his ears still seemed to work just fine. Whoever was outside the door really wanted in. Endless rounds fired at the door. It wouldn't take them long to shoot their way through.

Sullivan reached the grate. It was a far drop to the bottom. "Man, can you climb down this ladder?"

Connor pulled his legs under him tried to push himself up, but the pain in his arm was too great. Fresh blood soaked through Sullivan's shirt. He shook his head no and fell back to the floor.

"Okay, this is gonna hurt." Sullivan shook his head.

"Just do it before I pass out. Help me to the opening." Their only hope of survival was to drop Connor through and hope Charlotte could heal the damage. Connor put his feet through first, leaning on Sullivan for support. Connor nodded, giving the go-ahead for Sullivan to push. Connor fell with a thud. Sullivan slipped in behind him just as the door to the room was blown off its hinges.

Sullivan skipped the first several steps and almost fell off the ladder. He pulled the grate shut behind him, locking it from the inside.

"Quick, over here." Katrina was close. They couldn't see her through all the darkness, but her voice was loud. Sullivan scooped Connor up from behind, wrapped his arms around Connor's chest and dragged him along.

Following the direction of Katrina's voice, they made their way to the doorway where Katrina and Charlotte waited. Katrina swung the door shut and turned the lever before anyone was able to break open the grate.

"Where's Char?" Sullivan yelled.

"I'm right here." Charlotte hugged him and was nearly blinded when Katrina lit the lantern she pulled out of her bag.

"Connor's been shot," he said. Katrina was already inspecting his wounds. "You have to heal him."

"I think his leg is broken too," Katrina said. "Or at least cut pretty bad."

"I'm sorry. I had to push him through." Sullivan knelt next to him. "He couldn't climb down."

"It's okay. I can fix it." Charlotte leaned down and picked up Connor's arm. She straightened out his leg and he let out a loud groan. He tensed his body. He wasn't prepared for the pain overwhelming him. Charlotte pressed her hands hard against his skin, sending a heat as hot as boiling water through his skin and into his bones. He screamed, unable to refrain from crying out as her magic worked the bones in his leg back together. As soon as she removed her hands, the pain vanished and his body relaxed.

"Not done yet, Connor." Charlotte ran her other hand through his hair. "Catch your breath. When you're ready, I've gotta heal your arm."

"Just do it." He struggled to breathe; his body now covered in sweat. As much as he wanted to rest before the pain began again, he knew they weren't safe here. It wouldn't take those soldiers long to break through the grate and discover this door. Even if they decided to search the tunnels, his screams would lead them to their hiding spot. He winced when Charlotte pressed her hands onto his arm. The same burning heat that shot through his leg now rushed through his arm, seeking out every injured inch of his body.

"Almost done. Be thankful the bullet went clean through or this would be worse." Connor's breathing slowed as the bullet wound in his arm healed. Just as the bones in his leg had melded into one again, the hole in his arm knitted back together as if it never happened.

"See, all done." Charlotte smiled at him.

His breathing returned to normal and the sweat drenching his body began to dry. He slowly opened his eyes and smiled back at Charlotte.

"That's twice in two days." He wrapped his hand around

Charlotte's and let her pull him up to a seated position. "Your magic works fast."

"Take it easy. Not too fast." Katrina stood over him, next to Sullivan.

"I don't think now is the time to take it easy." Connor was up and standing. He wobbled from the dizziness in his head, but nothing he couldn't handle. He was in no danger of dying, none of them were, as long as they kept moving. "We better get out of here before they blow the lid off this place."

Katrina nodded and handed a flashlight to Connor. Without a word, she turned and took the lead. The others filed in behind her as they disappeared in the darkness of the tunnel.

CHAPTER FIVE

2031: Day 67, Friday

After an hour of walking through the cold, dark tunnel, the journey began to take its toll on the group. Their pace had slowed to a near crawl, especially Connor's. He should have rested for a while before walking on his newly healed leg, but there had been no time. They had to move quickly or else risk being found by the attackers and taken captive. Or worse, killed on the spot.

Charlotte tried to act as a crutch for Connor, but he refused her. He insisted even that would have been too slow. Instead, he forced himself to run with the rest of them until he was comfortable with the distance they'd put between them and the attackers.

They remained in silence most of the journey. Connor sensed Sullivan had something he wanted to say but didn't, either out of fear of whatever was eating away at him or out of sheer tiredness. Connor couldn't quite get a read on him in the darkness. He almost asked him several times what was wrong, but decided to let it go. Sullivan had been through too much, they all had. He'd speak when he was ready.

Connor suspected he already knew what it was that ate away at Sullivan's thoughts. He'd tried to tell them before Connor forced them out through the escape tunnel. Somehow Sullivan knew it was SUM attacking headquarters. He knew they were coming before they fired their first weapon. It might have had something to do with the device implanted in Sullivan's neck. If that was true, Sullivan's silence only meant one thing. He blamed himself for the attack.

"We're almost there." Katrina led them through the abandoned tunnels of the subway to an emergency meeting location. It was a couple miles away from headquarters, hidden below the city. They rounded a corner and were stopped by two large metal double doors marking the entrance of the secret meeting location. Five guards stepped out of the shadows, immediately brought their guns up, and aimed at them.

"Code 47288, Katrina Hicks and Connor Vance," Katrina called out before they could fire.

"Code 27488, second verification," one of the guards answered.

"Code 74882," Connor replied.

The guards lowered their guns and stepped aside, letting them pass. Connor couldn't help but chuckle at seeing his emergency plan in action. The lengthy security codes had been his idea. An idea Marc had argued against and insisted was overkill. If Marc made it out alive, he'd probably be the first to shoot if someone tried to enter without a code, even if he knew who they were.

The doors opened to a large, single room with a long table in the center surrounded by a few chairs. The light in the room was dim, making it hard to see, but Connor saw several bunk beds lined against the back wall. There was also a small kitchen and floor to ceiling shelves well stocked with supplies along the wall to the right. He'd never been to this hideout before and was glad to see it was well taken care of in case of a situation just like this.

"Katrina, Connor." Elle smiled. "Glad to see you made it out alive. Is anyone else with you?" Connor was surprised she sounded happy to see them.

"No, just us," Katrina said. "Is this all that made it out? How many?"

"Twenty here at this location." Elle dropped her smile. "But there's a chance some made it to the south and central holdings. We've no way to communicate at the moment to know for sure."

"Twenty." Connor searched the room; certain Elle must be wrong. "But that's not enough."

"We had no warning," Elle continued. "By the time an alarm was tripped, we were under full attack. There was no time for an ordered evacuation."

"What about Silka and Marc?" Connor looked around the room and didn't see either of them.

"No such luck getting rid of me." Marc sat up from one of the top bunks along the back wall. His eyes were red and burned with hatred. He looked like he'd been crying, but Connor couldn't say for sure. "But I'm afraid Silka wasn't as lucky."

Marc pointed to Silka's body lying on the bunk below him, her body limp and motionless. Charlotte ran up to her and took her hand. Connor helped Charlotte roll her over and laid her flat on her back. Silka's shirt was soaked in blood as was the sheets and blankets around her. Ripping her shirt open, she had two gunshot wounds in the chest. The wounds still bled. Connor felt for a pulse but found none.

"Can you save her?" Connor whispered. He felt no life in her, but Charlotte said she'd saved animals whose hearts stopped.

"She's not gone yet." Charlotte laid her hands on top of the wounds, one on each, and pressed down. A white glow formed around her hands where they met Silka's body.

"Get off her, she's dead." Marc jumped off the top bunk and lunged for Charlotte's arm, but Connor blocked his reach.

"There's still life in her," Charlotte whispered. "I feel it pulsing through her veins." She held her hands steady and pressed harder. The white glow spread across Silka's chest until her entire midsection lit up the room and drowned out the darkness. Charlotte's body stiffened, strained by the pull on her magic. A wave of energy washed across the room, strong enough for everyone to feel, and whirled around Charlotte's body. Pulling the energy inward, she concentrated it at her hands. With one forceful push, a pump on Silka's chest, all the energy rushed into Silka's wounds. A minute of silence passed, maybe two, and Charlotte held steady. The glow of her power never wavered, not for a second. Charlotte's magic found the bullets lodged inside Silka and pushed them to the surface until they were out. Silka sucked in a deep breath of air and her chest heaved out. Charlotte held her hands tight, straining her own body to hold Silka in place as her legs and arms began to flail.

"Just a minute longer, Silka," Charlotte called out, and Silka stilled. Every eye in the room was on them, focused on Charlotte's hands and the magic flowing through her. A thin stream of blood ran from Charlotte's nose and dripped onto the ends of her long blonde braid. Her legs trembled and her body was close to exhaustion.

"Not yet," Charlotte called out. Connor placed a hand on her shoulder and pulled on his own magic for support. He couldn't heal Silka, but he could lend Charlotte his magical strength, help her finish this task. It was the boost she needed. Charlotte mastered her body and all signs of exhaustion left her. A bright burst of light shot in all directions from Charlotte's hands, knocking Connor away. She fell to the floor, her body spent.

Silka's body shifted on the bed and she opened her eyes, the two bullet holes in her chest gone. The only evidence they existed was the blood covering her and the sheets.

"Oh my God." Marc's jaw dropped. "I don't believe it. How did you do that?" He pulled a blanket from his top bunk and wrapped it around Silka. He held her tight, tears running down his face.

"My... my power." Charlotte was hunched over, resting on her hands and knees. Connor, Katrina, and Sullivan huddled around her, each with a hand on her. All the magic and power they had concentrated on Charlotte, settling her nerves and replenishing her well, if only just enough to keep her from passing out. "I can heal wounds and give life back to the dead, assuming too much time hasn't passed."

"Silka," Marc whispered. "You're alive."

The room was silent, no one dared move. A bright light from their combined magic remained, sustained in midair. Connor scanned the group and frowned. Elle and Marc stared at Silka, both stunned and amazed at what they witnessed. *Now they see the truth.* The truth Connor tried to tell them earlier today when they wouldn't listen. Now that it was too late, they'd lost headquarters, and countless were dead, they believed.

"But, she died on the way here," Elle declared. "How is this possible?"

"This is what I tried to tell you," Connor said. "Our powers are enhanced. Charlotte can heal."

"Look, I'll show you." Charlotte stood next to Marc. Her

legs were still weak but her nose appeared to stop bleeding. She reached her hands out in front of her, palms up. Soft, white light began to seep out of her hands. Faint at first, but within seconds the white glow concentrated into a bright ball. The light illuminating from her hands lit up the room again. She looked up at Marc, his eyes wide and his mouth open. "It's okay, Marc. This is life, I am life. This is the gift that SUM gave me."

"But how?" He shook his head and backed away from her.

She shrugged her shoulders. "Honestly, no clue. I'm not sure they even knew what they were giving me, or any of us when they did this."

Charlotte looked around the room, every eye was on her. The last remaining members of the Order of Peace stood waiting for her to explain her existence, Sullivan's existence, and why they were so different. Connor should have been pleased they were finally listening, but nothing but anger built up inside him.

"All we know is we were bred in a laboratory," she said, pointing behind her to Connor, Katrina, and Sullivan. "SUM took seeds from some of the most powerful Magical Bond at the time and fertilized eggs in the lab. They experimented until we were the result."

"I don't understand," Elle said. "How did that make your magic different?"

"SUM has been trying to develop an enhancement drug for years, but nothing has worked." Connor stepped next to Charlotte, checking his anger. Now he had their attention and he'd do his best to get them to understand everything. "If you all saw even a fraction of what I saw on that island, you would've already tried to destroy every one of them. They are trying to make a drug to cure the Common Blood, but everything they've ever tried has failed. They keep killing innocent people to test new theories and drugs. The only thing that has worked is us. They encoded our genes with some type of enhancement drug during fetal development. We are the result of that experiment."

The group was dazed. The range of emotions was too intense to get a good handle on the crowd. Most were still trying to wrap their minds around what Charlotte had done and now Connor dumped this information on them as well.

"How many of you are there?" Marc finally broke the silence. His look of confusion shifted to anger.

"We're the only ones we are aware of," Connor answered. "And Ebony, but she didn't make it out."

"Is she dead?" Elle asked.

"No." Connor shook his head and dread filled his heart. He tried his best to not think about Ebony, about what could be happening to her. His only hope was her strength in her magic. She was stronger than anything Dr. Hunter could possibly have planned for her. "At least I don't think so, but I do fear what Dr. Hunter may have planned for her. Whatever it is, it isn't good."

"Who's he?" Marc practically barked out the words. His question further proving he hadn't been listening to Connor earlier.

"Her father. Dr. Daniel Hunter," Connor continued. "He's the mastermind behind everything SUM has been doing."

"There could be more of you working for him then?" Elle dropped back into the chair, her head hung low.

"There could be, but not on the island," Charlotte answered. "If more like us exist, they were bred and raised somewhere else."

"How do you know?" Marc threw a harsh look at her, his body tensed. Whatever awe he felt for Charlotte for saving

Silka's life was gone now.

"The island is small," she said. "The institution wasn't large enough to hide more of us. We would've known they were there."

"Guys, we could talk about this all day," Sullivan interrupted. His hands were shaking and a thin line of sweat beaded up above his top lip. "But I need to get out of here. I'm not safe."

"What are you talking about?" Charlotte asked. "We got away. SUM won't find us here."

"That's not what I mean." Fear washed over his face. Connor knew what he was about to say before he spoke the words. "I think I am the reason SUM found your headquarters."

"The control device they implanted in you." Connor dropped his head.

"Yep, and it's still in my neck, man." Sullivan reached up and rubbed the spot where it had been injected. "I felt it right before they started firing on us."

"It's a tracker," Connor said. "Damn it. I was affraid of that?"

"You mean you led them right to us?" Marc yelled right before he lunged himself towards Sullivan. Connor blocked his path and grabbed him before he reached Sullivan

Sullivan remained motionless, his face blank. "I gotta get outta here and away from all of you before it happens again."

"No," Charlotte grabbed his hand. "Where you go, I go too."

"You need to stay with them." Sullivan pulled her close and gave her a tight hug. "They could use your help. Plus, I can't let SUM get to you."

The mood in the room suddenly became very clear to

Connor's senses. Fear. Every person in the room was afraid that SUM would shoot down the door any minute, including himself. Even Marc relaxed and stepped back from Sullivan on his own. If Connor didn't figure out a way to control this fear, and fast, the entire group might turn on each other and start running away. Their best chance at survival was sticking together.

"I'll take him to get it removed." Connor nodded at Sullivan and forced a smile. "We'll leave right now."

"I'm going, too." Charlotte stepped in front of Sullivan, fighting back the tears.

"No," Sullivan pushed her back and set her down on the bed next to Silka. "You need to stay with them. Your magic is more valuable to them than to me."

She shook her head no, ready to protest.

"Look, Char," Connor said, "we'll move fast, and we'll stay low. I know where I'm going. SUM has no clue how to maneuver the Levels. That works to our advantage."

"I don't like it." Charlotte struggled to hold back the tears.

"Diesel?" Katrina asked, her fear replaced with anger.

"Yeah, he can do this." Connor squeezed her hand.

She turned her back to him so he couldn't see the tears welling up in her eyes. Diesel was no friend to Katrina, to any of them, but he was the best surgeon they knew.

Connor picked up the bags they'd brought with them from headquarters and dug around to check for ammo. "He owes me one anyway. We'll be back before you know it."

"Come on." Sullivan grabbed Connor's arm, pulling him towards the door. "I've stayed here too long already. We have to keep movin'."

Sullivan hugged his sister one last time before helping

Connor gather more supplies. They had enough food for three days, plenty of ammo, and a couple of extra guns. In unison, they turned and nodded at Katrina and Charlotte before leaving and following the tunnels out into the city.

CHAPTER SIX

2031: Day 68, Saturday Early Morning

Morning was upon them, and Katrina hadn't slept all night. She had no way of checking the time. There were no clocks she could find and no windows to watch for the sunrise, but her internal clock told her it was time to get up.

As hard as she tried to drift off into a deep sleep, she couldn't. Her worry over Connor and Sullivan made it impossible to relax enough to let sleep take over. The mention of Diesel's name didn't help either. It brought back memories that haunted her thoughts. It had been years since she last saw him, since his actions and poor judgment resulted in the death of her best friend. She tried over the years to let it go, to forgive Diesel, but there were some wrong doings that can never be forgotten, and some harder still to forgive.

She wasn't the only one awake. Two dim floodlights provided just enough light to see the movements of others. A few hours ago, the security detail switched shifts and those who came in never managed to find sleep either. Whether it was their own worry, or the random flicker of the lights keeping them awake, she didn't know. The occasional rattle of the walls certainly didn't help.

Something bad was happening on the surface and it fed her worry even more. The three stories of rock, dirt, and concrete between them and the surface muffled the noise, but every rattle of the walls followed a distant boom. That boom made it impossible to relax and rest.

Instead of sleep, she laid on the top bunk and listened. She listened to the soft breathing of Charlotte sleeping below her, the vibration of Marc's deep snore in the bunk next to her, and the whispers of the few she didn't know on the other side of the room.

Katrina knew less than ten of the people who made it out and reached this holding location. Outside of the council members and Charlotte, there were only two others she recognized. So many of her friends, or former friends it would seem, weren't here. The Order had three emergency evacuation hideouts for situations like this. If the other two locations had no more survivors than here, chances were most of the people she cared about didn't make it to safety. Headquarters housed about three hundred members and with only twenty here, the odds didn't look good.

She rolled over hoping a change in position would help her find sleep, but instead found herself with a direct view of a man she had never seen before. He was talking to three of the guards who had met them outside when they arrived. She didn't think he had been guarding the entrance with them, but she could be wrong.

Something about him caught her attention. He was handsome enough, but that wasn't it. His dark brown hair was clean cut, tight around his neck and a little longer on top. He had a gentle smile. She couldn't see the color of his eyes in this light, but she sensed a kindness unlike anything she had ever detected before. At least she thought it was kindness. Being this tired, her magic sometimes failed her. He glanced in her direction and caught her staring. His gentle smile grew into laughter. She quickly rolled over, embarrassed.

Another boom, louder than the others, caused her to sit up in bed. The room fell silent except the rattle of the walls and the faint sound of tiny rocks rolling above her head. That had been closer, much closer than the others she heard. Not only did she hear it, but it shook her bones like it was right on top of them. A few moments passed, and Marc's snoring started up again. Whatever caused the boom, it hadn't been enough to wake him or the others.

Katrina stared at the ceiling and listened. Silence came from above and she heard nothing but the whispers and snores in the room. Despite the silence from above, she sensed something was coming. *Was that a faint rumble? Or the pounding of feet running in the distance?* She couldn't quite make sense of it or focus in on what it was, but something was there. She was certain.

She scanned the room, looking to the others who were awake. They didn't seem to notice a thing.

Her head jerked towards the door. *Was that a gunshot?* She could've sworn she heard a gun fire. Listening carefully, she dared not breathe. All she could hear was Marc's muffled snore and the faint whisper of the men on the other side of the room. She wanted to yell at them to be silent, but she didn't want to cause unnecessary panic. She wasn't convinced she had heard anything.

So, she waited in silence. Barely breathing, she watched the door.

A rustling sound. A faint drag or scrape.

She leaned forward, concentrating on blocking out the sounds of the room and listening for anything beyond these walls. The harder she concentrated, the more definite the silence became.

A click.

Either she was losing her mind, or someone who didn't belong there was outside those doors. She slid off the bunk and started for the door. The hair on the back of her neck tingled and a nervousness that made her want to vomit settled in her gut.

"Hey, Katrina, right?" The man who caught her staring called her name and she shifted her attention in his direction. "That's your name, isn't it?"

"Yeah." She nodded. Her breathing quickened and her magic was on full alert. Her head was about to burst into flames. She was too tired to control the warnings her magic called out to her.

"Are you ok—"

A deafening boom exploded into the room, throwing Katrina between the rows of bunk beds until her body slammed against the back wall. Whatever light was provided in the room was shadowed by a haze of dust and rock. Large rocks, boulders of concrete, crumbled from above, smashing the bunks before her.

She called out for Charlotte, but the sound of crashing rock drowned out her voice. She couldn't hear her own screams.

Heavy. Her body felt heavy, she couldn't move her arms or legs.

Darkness. Complete darkness consumed her as she fell into the deep sleep her body had denied her earlier.

THE DISTANT SOUND OF VOICES BROUGHT her back to the moment. Katrina blinked several times, her eyelids heavy and her lashes pasted together. The spray from a nearby busted water pipe turned the layer of dust settled on her into a thick paste. She tried to wipe her face clean of it, but her arm was trapped. Wiggling her fingers, she freed her hand, but a large chunk of concrete had fallen on top her and held her arm close to her body. She shifted slightly to her side, just enough to create an open space between her body and the floor. The space was tight, but her left arm was now free to wipe her eyes. Even after wiping her eyes clean, it was still hard to see. Dust filled the air and her face was covered again.

 She blinked several times, trying to make sense of her surroundings. She focused her eyes on the movement beyond the haze in front of her. There were several people searching the rubble, but she couldn't see well enough to know who they were. She started to call out for help but froze when she felt a power surge from across the room. Someone with great magical ability was near. Someone who meant to cause them harm. SUM had found them.

 A light breeze tickled across her face and within moments the dust-filled air was clear. The figures she saw in the haze were SUM soldiers searching for bodies—searching for them.

 Katrina kept her head low and scooted back under the rock. The concrete rubble hid her body and with any luck, they wouldn't find her. She shifted her eyes around the room looking for anyone. Her eyes drifted to where her bunk had been. The bunks they slept in were still intact and standing, but she saw no signs of Charlotte. A little more to the left and her eyes met the dark, lifeless stare of Marc. His eyes were empty, his body crushed beneath the ceiling that fell from above.

 Dead.

 Silka had been below him. She focused on the rubble

around Marc, looking for any sign of another body but found none. Unlike Katrina's bunk, their bunk was crushed and there was too much debris to tell what was there.

A scream pulled her attention away from the pile of rubble near Marc and she darted her eyes around the room. She settled her attention on a couple guards tossing rock and concrete to the side not far from her bunk bed. An arm—they were pulling at an arm. Another scream in protest.

Words were spoken on the other side of the room but before she could make sense of what they were, Charlotte stood before the guards, her long blonde hair gray with dust and a trickle of blood running down her arm.

More words, commands, came from the powerful figure in the doorway. Katrina dropped her head behind the concrete slab that hid her body and focused her power on the figure commanding the guards to search the room. The man's power was strong, too strong for her to sense who he was. Her magic, her body, was too weak.

The guards bounded Charlotte's hands and pulled her towards the doorway. Katrina watched Charlotte kick at the guards, but it had done her no good. The foreign power in the room seized her body and Charlotte collapsed, unable to control her movements. The guards dragged her out of sight.

Katrina tucked her head as far under the concrete slab as she could, hoping it would be enough to conceal her location. Moments later she heard the distant command to roll out. The rustling sound of their feet faded into the distance and she was left alone. No snoring, no soft breathing of sleep, and no whispers from the small group across the room. Only her own breathing and the faint hiss of water from the busted pipe spraying on her face.

KATRINA HAD FALLEN ASLEEP, or passed out, after the guards cleared the room. She still had no sense of how much time passed. She didn't know how it was possible, but she could now move her legs and both arms. The heavy weight that held her down was gone. The large slab of concrete had been moved aside. But how?

She was not alone. Someone, maybe more than one person, was with her in the room. Fear, followed by panic, washed over her and she tried to make herself small. Maybe if she curled into a tight ball, whoever it was that moved the slab would not see her.

She held her breath and dared not open her eyes to look. But it was too late. A gentle hand rested on the arm that was pinned.

"You okay?" A man's voice. She didn't recognize the voice, but it was soft and caring. "Katrina, can you hear me?"

He knew her name. Whoever this was, he knew her despite the dust and small bits of gravel covering her body. A random guard would not recognize her in this state, even if he had seen her before. She slowly opened her eyes, peeling away the plastered dust on her face. Her eyelids were heavy and her vision unfocused. The man gently wiped away the remaining grit and dirt. Blinking a few times, her eyes focused. The handsome man who had caught her staring sat before her.

"Anything broken?" He scanned her arms and legs before returning his eyes to hers. "Can you get up?"

"I think so," she answered, her voice rough from breathing in dust.

"We seem to be it. I suggest we get out of here before they return." He took her hand and helped her stand. She stumbled backward. Her legs were stiff and her back ached. It took her a moment to catch her balance. It was like she hadn't stood in days, maybe even weeks. How long had she been trapped under there, her body crushed by the weight of the concrete? And how did he manage to free her from her trap? She held her eyes on his, attempting to read his intentions. He was Magical Bond, and strong.

"My magic," he said. He sensed her hesitation. "My magic is stronger than most. It was a struggle, but it was enough to free you."

He tugged at her hand and nodded towards the exit. Katrina looked around the room once more. No other survivors remained. "No one else made it," she whispered.

"No." He turned to her; his voice solemn. "They took a couple survivors with them, but I didn't see who they were."

"Charlotte. They got Charlotte." She pulled her hand free of his and walked towards Marc's body. Much of the rubble covering his body had been removed she assumed by this stranger, but it could have been by the guards before they left. The removal revealed the body of her friends, Silka and Elle, both crushed not far from Marc.

How had she survived this, or Charlotte, or this stranger for that matter? Had it been their magic that saved them? Katrina leaned down and picked up Silka's hand, it was cold and lifeless. The tiny bit of magic Silka possessed had not been enough to save her life.

"Katrina," he called. "I know they were your friends, but we really should go."

She placed Silka's hand on her chest where her heart once beat. When she stood, her legs trembled, and she fell backward into the stranger's arms. She pushed away from him, slapping his hands away as she stumbled free. She fell again. Her body was too weak to make it on her own and she couldn't force her legs to carry her weight no matter how hard she tried.

"It's okay." The man scooped her up in his arms as if

she weighed nothing. He was strong, both physically and magically. She wanted to fight his hold on her, to walk on her own. But she had not the strength to even squirm herself free.

"I've got you," he whispered in her ear, his lips so close they brushed against her skin. She dropped her head onto his shoulder and drifted out of consciousness.

CHAPTER SEVEN

2031: Day 68, Saturday

Connor and Sullivan's journey to find Diesel had been much more difficult than Connor anticipated. The forces that attacked headquarters had not stopped there. Soldiers searched every building, every home, every possible hiding place they could find looking for resistance—looking for the Order. They were all being hunted by SUM. Every last Order member was being snuffed out and either killed on the spot or taken captive.

They were unable to walk in the open and had to quickly move from shadow to shadow. Often, they would detour to the less-traveled alleys that required them to climb over buildings or hop fences. They didn't make it far before they were forced to hide in a sewer drain under the city streets.

Government soldiers crowded the streets, marching in all directions and standing guard at every major intersection. This only reinforced Connor's concerns that SUM controlled the government and that whatever support SUM needed,

SUM was going to get.

Near dusk, Connor ventured out of their hiding place below the city and found most of the soldiers were gone. Only a few stood guard at the major intersections. Whatever hunt they had been on last night, had been completed and they called off most of the search, at least for the time being.

Connor and Sullivan resumed their travels, doing their best to stay out of sight. They didn't have far to go to reach the Levels, but Connor worried they were still being tracked by that thing in Sullivan's neck. Yet, no one had come close to finding them last. Maybe they were both wrong, it didn't double as a tracker, and SUM had found headquarters another way.

Regardless, they couldn't risk getting caught. If they were taken hostage, that would be it for them. There was no way Dr. Hunter would let them escape twice and all hope of saving Ebony would be crushed.

They stopped to rest in a quiet alley. Signs of civilization faded the farther they traveled away from the hideout, making it easier for them to move. Connor still moved with caution and assumed eyes were watching. He continued to look for any sign of them.

"We're getting close." Connor opened one of their bags and tossed Sullivan a bottle of water. "Drink. This will be our last chance for a break until we reach Diesel's house. Better eat, too."

Neither of them had been hungry when they left their early-morning hiding spot, but now Connor was famished. He handed Sullivan a breakfast bar and they ate in silence.

"How much further?" Sullivan drank the last of his water before stuffing it in his bag.

"A couple blocks, maybe," Connor said. He could see the exhaustion and worry on Sullivan's face, maybe even a little guilt. "I'm sure the girls are fine."

Sullivan shrugged, avoiding Connor's stare. "Can this guy really help?"

"Diesel?" Connor pulled a can of peaches out of his bag and handed it to Sullivan, but he refused. Connor popped the top and stuffed a few pieces in his mouth. "Diesel is a brilliant doctor. He used to be the best we had."

"What do you mean, used to?" Sullivan shot him a questioning look.

"Well, where to begin? Diesel has a lot of problems, mostly gambling, and partly drugs. After the war, life was tough for Common Blood. He struggled to maintain his status. He got mixed in with the wrong crowd and piled up a debt he would never be able to repay. He lost his job at the hospital when a few gangsters showed up and broke both his arms for missing a debt payment. That's how his wife found out about the gambling. She left him, took everything he had besides money because he didn't have any left. It was a shame really, he was the best."

"And this is who you're taking me to?" Sullivan asked. "He sounds like a real loser."

"Everybody has their problems." Connor smiled. "That doesn't make them bad at their jobs. He's the only one I'd trust to take that thing out. Yes, he's a little rough around the edges, and he may try to kill me when we show up, but if anyone can do this, it's him."

CONNOR LEFT SULLIVAN IN A DECREPIT building across the street from Diesel's home, if you could call where Diesel lived a home. Diesel lived in the Levels where so many other Common Blood were forced to live—in the remnants of the fallen down buildings and rubble left from the aftermath of war. The Levels were once a thriving community of homes and business spanning from the central reaches of the Bronx, across Harlem River, and all of what was once known as Harlem. Connor never spent much time in the Bronx or Harlem before the war flattened the area, but it had been home to so many. He glanced behind him at the building where Sullivan waited. The rundown building looked more stable than the one he was about to enter.

Diesel's home only had three walls and a partial roof. It was about eight or nine blocks east of the Central Park boundary. This area fared better than across the river in the Bronx where dozens of blocks were flattened for miles. Still, one side of Diesel's building had been blown off when the building next to it took a direct hit from a bomb. The door to the front entrance did not survive the war, either, and it was an unprotected opening that led to a filthy, dark room. Connor stepped inside on silent feet and waited, listening for any signs of life. The foyer was still covered in black dust from the explosion more than ten years ago. Connor thought being exposed to the elements would've washed some of the filth away, but instead, it looked perfectly preserved, as if the building refused to let the memory fade. He could still smell smoldering ash from the fire that blazed through, but now a sour smell of death and rot was layered on top.

Connor didn't expect to be greeted with joy and saw no need to expose Sullivan to another potential threat. Facing Diesel alone was the only way to neutralize him and convince him to help. He slowly moved to the bottom of the stairs and waited; gun aimed up. By some miracle, the second floor remained intact, at least most of it. A few rotted floorboards exposed the second floor from below but nothing that couldn't be easily maneuvered by stepping around or over it. The stairs were on the opposite side of the building, protected from the blast of the explosion. Connor advanced, soft on his feet, making his way up the stairs. With each step, he paused and studied his surroundings. Knowing Diesel, he was prepared for intruders. Connor needed to proceed with caution and keep an eye out for Diesel's traps.

Diesel didn't like unannounced visitors, and he wasn't a fan of Connor. The last run in between Connor and him ended in a death threat. Diesel had started dealing drugs after he lost his position at the hospital. When the Order found out, they arrested Diesel. It wasn't a real arrest since the Order had no legal authority, but it was enough to establish boundaries and expectations in their world.

Connor placed his foot on the next step and saw the wire a second too late.

"Shit," he whispered and quickly shifted his body to the right so he was hidden from the view above. He heard a faint whine from the alarm he set off when he stepped on the wire. Diesel now knew someone was coming up the stairs.

Connor heard Diesel scrambling, most likely arming himself against the intruder. If Connor remembered correctly, these stairs were the only way in and out. Diesel had nowhere to go.

"Diesel," Connor yelled up the stairs. "It's Connor Vance. I need your help."

Connor heard a loud thump, but no answer. It had been over three years since the Order banished Diesel to the Levels for his refusal to stop dealing drugs. Connor knew better than to assume Diesel would no longer hold a grudge against him for the Order's decision. It had been a lucrative opportunity for Diesel and those are hard to come by for Common Blood, even talented doctors like him.

They needed doctors, desperately. But unlike dealing drugs, there was no money to be made as a doctor unless you were appointed to one of the major hospitals by the Board of Medicine. And since the government controlled the Board of Medicine, Common Blood citizens were never appointed to the high paying jobs no matter how talented they were. Only the rich and powerful could afford to be treated by the government-sanctioned hospitals, leaving most without medical care. Diesel's talents could have served the Order well, but greed won him over and left him cast out of all decent society.

"Diesel," Connor called out, before taking another step up. "We need your help."

"Why should I help you, asshole?" Diesel yelled.

Connor smiled. He was talking. Talking was a good sign.

"Because you hate SUM more than you hate me." The smile on Connor's face grew and he fought to hold back his chuckle. If he could see Diesel's face, he knew it would give away his true feelings. Diesel's real anger was at SUM, always had been. He used his frustration with the Order as a substitute outlet for his anger. "You've always wanted to fight in this battle. Now's your chance."

Silence. Connor took a few more steps up towards the second floor. A door hinge creaked, but was it opening or closing? Connor watched each step he took more closely than before. He could almost see the landing now.

Silence.

Two more steps.

Connor peaked around the final corner where the stairs turned for the last few steps before meeting the second floor. An open door was just at the corner. Still no sign of Diesel. With his gun aimed and ready, and pausing with each movement of his feet, Connor took his time with the last ten steps before reaching the landing.

Still no movements. No sounds.

Connor continued making his way to the door with slow, quiet steps. The room was dark, and he couldn't see the shape of a body anywhere. The faint hint of smoke suggested a candle or two may have been lit before he triggered the alarm. Connor placed one foot inside the door, the floor below creaked and bowed beneath his feet. Pulling back, he hunched down next to the door and waited.

"Diesel?" he called out. "Does this mean I can come in? Without a fight?"

Connor waited; his ear held close to the open door. Nothing. Not even the sound of a body shifting in its seat. "Come on, Diesel. I don't have time for games. Please, may I come in?"

"Yeah," a grumpy voice responded from within. "I don't have the energy to fight you anyway."

Connor stood and took a step into the door. The same floorboard gave way and he jumped back. He scooted his foot forward to the next board and the same thing happened. This was another one of Diesel's traps. If he put his weight on these boards, he'd crash through to the floor below.

"It's all or nothing, Connor." Diesel let out a deep bellowing laugh. "You're going to have to jump in."

Connor took a step back and leaped forward, rolling across the floor and landing in a squat position, gun pointed in the direction of Diesel's voice. Diesel sat on a sofa against the wall, a gun resting on his knee and aimed directly at Connor's head.

"Jeez, Diesel." Connor coughed, fighting back the urge to gag. The sour smell of rot concentrated in this room. "When's the last time you showered?"

"Well," Diesel said, letting out a laugh, "you don't look so great yourself." He leaned forward and lifted his gun, causing Connor to jerk and cock his own gun. Diesel smiled, held his hand up, and slowly put his gun on the table next to the sofa.

"Maybe," Connor sighed and dropped his gun to his side, being sure to leave it cocked. "But I definitely smell better."

Diesel glanced at Connor's gun before holding his stare. "Unlike you, I don't have running water."

"Maybe you should move." Connor looked around at the state of his living conditions. The streets had to be cleaner than this place.

"As I recall," Diesel said, "someone cut off my primary cash flow and pushed me into this hell hole."

"We couldn't let you continue down that path, and you know it."

"That's your opinion." Diesel leaned back on the sofa and spread his arms over the back and smiled. Diesel was a proud man and never saw anything wrong with what he did. Diesel, just like so many, was trying to survive by any means possible.

"You have other skills." Connor stepped backward, firmly placing each foot down one at a time, checking the stability of the floorboards. He glanced around the corner and into the next room. "Much more valuable skills than drug dealing."

"I'm alone. You can relax." Diesel smiled.

Connor stiffened at his devious smile. He knew chances were high Diesel was alone, but he wasn't about to let his guard down. He needed this man's help and he wouldn't get it unless he relaxed, even if it was only for show. Connor decocked the hammer of the gun and slid it into the holster on his belt.

"We could use a doctor," Connor said, deciding to get to the point of his visit.

"Nobody wants a doctor, jackass. They want drugs." Diesel jumped up out of his seat and pushed Connor up against the wall. He held a knife to Connor's throat. "Give me one good reason why I shouldn't end you now."

Connor stared Diesel dead in the eyes, daring him to do it. It was hard to believe the man before him had once been the most respected surgeon in the city. If Connor didn't know better, he'd never believe it. Diesel looked like a worthless piece of shit that didn't deserve a life, even in this hell hole.

"Go ahead." Connor gave a slight nod. "If you think killing me will make you feel better, then do it."

"Maybe it will." He tightened his grip on Connor and pressed the knife into his neck until it cut a thin slice on the surface of his skin.

"I'm not the enemy and you know it." Connor didn't flinch, didn't look the least bit concerned that Diesel could end his life in a split second.

"Seeing you dead will still make me feel better." Diesel spat in his face.

"Then why am I still alive?" Connor kept his voice calm, never broke a sweat.

"Good question." He held his stare but still didn't move in for the kill. Connor let out a shallow laugh.

"You're not going to kill me. So back off." Connor's smile grew. "We have more important things to discuss than your hatred for me."

"Says you," Diesel said in a forced gruff, attempting to hide the slight quiver in his voice.

Connor saw the slightest hesitation in Diesel's eyes and shoved his arm up between his neck and the knife. He kicked his leg around Diesel's legs and grabbed the knife from his hand as he went tumbling to the ground. Diesel was flat on his back in a matter of seconds. Connor smiled and stepped over him.

"I had hoped we could do this the easy way." Connor

reached behind his back and unfastened the rope attached to his belt. "If you insist on being difficult, I'll gladly tie you up and drag your ass out of here."

"Just tell me what it is you want." Diesel let his body relax into the floor.

"I need you to remove a sensor from a friend's neck," Connor said, his voice calm and even. "A control device that may double as a tracker."

"I can't do that, are you crazy?" Diesel stared at him; his eyes wild.

"You're the only option we have." Connor stepped over him and straddled his body. He grabbed his shirt and pulled his head close to his. "So, get up, pack your shit, and let's go."

Diesel held his stare and then spat in his face for the second time.

"Hard way it is." Connor wiped his face and grabbed Diesel's hands and started wrapping the rope around them. Before Diesel could attempt to fight back, Connor flipped him over and pulled the rope tight, locking his arms close to his body.

"Stop," Diesel yelled. "Fine, I'll go."

"Thank you." Connor loosened his hold on the rope and smiled.

"You're going to owe me big time for this one." Diesel sat up and unwrapped his hands.

"You make this work and we get out of this alive," Connor said, patting him on the back, "and I'll give you anything you want."

"Anything?" Diesel's devious smile returned.

"Within reason." Connor walked over to the door. "I'll go get my friend, then we can discuss a plan. We don't have a lot of time."

CHAPTER EIGHT

2031: Day 68, Saturday Evening

By the time Connor made it back to the entrance of Diesel's building with Sullivan, the sun had begun to set, and they were losing daylight fast. He couldn't stop himself from constantly checking his back, making certain no one was following them. The last thing he wanted was to lead SUM to Diesel. The man may be a serious pain in the ass, but he had his uses. Losing him to SUM would be bad. Plus, he was their only chance at getting this thing out of Sullivan's neck. Connor took each step up the stairs back to Diesel's apartment just as slow as he had the first time. Not because he was worried about the traps, but because without the sunlight, it was harder to see the rotted floorboards and strategically placed holes.

"This place is a nightmare." Sullivan watched Connor's movements closer and made certain only to step where he stepped. "No wonder it took you so long."

"Yeah, Diesel takes no chances. Plus, he needed some

convincing." Connor pointed at the open door after they rounded the corner. Diesel must have lit a candle because a soft light glowed beyond the doorway. Connor led Sullivan right to the door and stopped. "You're going to have to jump. See?" Connor pointed at the hole in the floor.

"That?" Sullivan's jaw dropped. The hole was at least four feet wide and the edges were jagged from where the floor was ripped out, not cut clean. "Dude, I can't make that."

"Sure you can." Connor smiled. "Just take a running jump. It's easier than it looks."

Sullivan stared at the hole in the floor. The darkness was so consuming it looked more like a bottomless pit to hell rather than an opening to the floor below.

"Don't listen to him." Diesel called from inside the apartment. "I can make it easy on you." A wide board slid across the hole creating a bridge for them to walk across. "Although, I suggest you cross quickly. My makeshift bridge could crack in the center and down you fall." He let out a deep bellowing laugh.

Connor slapped Sullivan on the shoulder. "Well, let's go." He smiled and took a running start to cross the makeshift bridge and in a matter of seconds, was on the other side. Sullivan hesitated, took a deep breath and took off. As soon as his first foot stepped on the board, his body wobbled, and he slowed down. This caused the board to shake and tilt slightly to one side. He balanced himself by placing his second foot down to flatten the board. Connor reached out and grabbed his arm, pulling him along and onto the stable surface of the floor on the other side.

Connor laughed as Sullivan regained his footing and tried to slow down his breathing. "Sully, meet Diesel. He'll do the surgery."

"Him?" Sullivan looked at Diesel, his eyes wide and his

breath quickened. "He doesn't look like he could hold a fork, let alone a scalpel."

"He may not look like much, but he's a good surgeon." Connor nodded at Diesel and took a seat on the sofa. He kicked his leg up, resting his ankle on his knee. Sullivan looked like he'd rather cut that thing out of his neck himself and Diesel looked pissed. Connor only smiled.

Diesel glared at both of them before placing his bag down on the table opposite the sofa. "Sit down," he demanded, pointing at the chair next to him. He lit another candle and the light in the room nearly doubled.

"What?" Sullivan looked at him, shaking his head no.

"Sit down now," Diesel repeated as he pulled a patch out of his bag.

"What is that?" Sullivan took a few steps backward.

"This will block the transmission of the tracker." Diesel's voice was harsh, his irritation growing. "Where is this damn thing?"

Sullivan turned his back towards him and pointed at his neck. "This red dot, right here."

"Sit," Diesel demanded again.

Sullivan complied. Diesel leaned down and wiped the spot with alcohol before attaching the patch. "This should adequately confuse them for a while, at least long enough for us to get to the hospital and get this thing out of you."

"Hospital?" Connor asked.

"Yeah." Diesel glanced over his shoulder at Connor like he was stupid. "Where did you think I was going to do this? Here, in this shit hole?"

Connor shrugged and looked around him. He hadn't considered where Diesel would do the surgery, only that he would do it. Like everything else going on in this world, he assumed there was some secret location where these things took place. This kind of procedure was just as illegal as dealing drugs. Those activities occurred on the streets or down dark alleys. He had assumed the same for illegal surgeries.

"Surgeries can't take place in the same places that drug deals go down," Diesel said, predicting what Connor was thinking. "It doesn't happen like that."

"I assumed—"

"That's your mistake." Diesel stood with his bag in hand and he slapped Sullivan on the back. "That should get us through. Let's go."

"Where?" Connor asked.

"Mount Sinai, just inside the boundary." Diesel shot across his makeshift bridge and waited for Connor and Sullivan to cross before he pulled the board over and hid it in a room down the hall. Mount Sinai was the last remaining surgical hospital in the city's center, fully run and operated by the Magical Bond. The Magical Bond now controlled all access to this hospital, along with all the buildings surrounding Central Park and large sections of Manhattan—at least the sections that remained.

Diesel skipped down the stairs much quicker than Connor was comfortable doing. By the time Connor and Sullivan joined him in the foyer he was tapping his foot with his arms folded across his chest. He headed out the door, the sky completely dark, and sprinted down the street heading east.

"Where are you going?" Connor called after him, pointing in the opposite direction. "Mount Sinai's this way."

"We can't exactly walk through the front door." Diesel laughed. "Come on, I know a back way in."

Connor let out a low growl. He wasn't pleased with this shift in control. He needed Diesel to comply, to do the surgery, but taking the lead was a different situation altogether.

Diesel led them down the street for two blocks before he turned down a narrow alley. With the night taking over, the streets started filling with the dopers and dealers. In many ways, the dopers could be more threatening than the dealers. Sure, the dealers had guns and other deadly weapons, but nothing could be more dangerous than a doper in desperate need of a fix. Except maybe a SUM soldier. At least Connor didn't see any soldiers patrolling the Levels. Even if SUM had tracked them here, they'd be hard pressed to find soldiers willing to search for them. No one wanted to be in the Levels, not even to hide.

Diesel opened a gate at the end of the alley and waved them through. Inside was an open grassy field, maybe an acre in size. Several trees surrounded the outer edge and along the remnant pathways within, but other than that it was an empty field, not a person or structure in sight. It was hard to see in the dark, but this park looked like it was spared during the bombing of the last war.

"No one should be able to follow us now," Diesel said. "Even if they had tracked him to my place, we should be safe."

He led them to the center of the field where a manhole was located. Diesel unlatched the top and lifted it. There was a second hatch door with a high-tech lock way too advanced for anything in the Levels. After he pushed a few buttons, it clicked and slowly rotated open, revealing a narrow tunnel with a ladder.

"Where did you get such a high-tech hatch and lock?" Connor stared in disbelief.

Diesel just smiled and pointed to the ladder. "Let's go, everybody in."

Sullivan went down first, followed by Connor and Diesel taking the rear. Once Diesel was in he pulled the cover shut and reengaged the locking mechanism. At the bottom of the ladder, Diesel opened a small cabinet door on the wall and pulled out a couple of flashlights.

"Here," he handed one to Connor. "It's not far down this tunnel, a mile or so."

"Where are you taking me?" Sullivan asked.

"To Mount Sinai Hospital," Diesel answered and proceeded down the narrow dark tunnel. The tunnel wasn't large enough for any of them to walk with their backs straight. They each had to hunch over slightly and walk single file.

"Yeah, but where exactly?" Sullivan called from the rear.

"Oh," Diesel glanced back at Sullivan with an apologetic look. "To the basements. There are old abandoned prep rooms down there that have running water, electricity and adequate light. This tunnel is a direct route. We should be safe."

"Are you sure everything still works down there?" Connor asked.

"Oh, yeah. I sneak over here often. This is where I shower." Anticipating Connor's snarky remark about his hygiene, he added, "Granted, it's been a few weeks since I was here, but I assure you, everything works."

They walked in silence for the next several minutes. The tunnel was completely dark and offered no light outside their flashlights. Connor didn't see any light fixtures on the walls or ceiling. Whatever this tunnel was used for, it was wet. There was a thick blanket of moisture in the air. Connor noted that his clothes were starting to feel damp and his hair stuck to his neck. Thankfully, there wasn't the foul odor of a typical sewer line which pleased Connor. He didn't like the idea of walking through shit.

"What is the tunnel used for?" Connor asked.

"Storm drains," Diesel answered. "When the ponds in Central Park fill, they dump into here. That overflow, along with the connecting street drains, enters this drainpipe and dumps right in the Harlem River."

"Well, that explains the moisture in the air," Sullivan mumbled.

"We're almost there. Right around this corner." Diesel led them to another ladder. He tossed his flashlight to Sullivan and climbed to the top. He punched in a code to a similarly advanced lock and hatch. It clicked open and he crawled through.

"Well." He stuck his head back in the manhole. "Are you coming?"

Diesel turned on the lights before Connor was able to step out of the manhole. The sudden brightness caused him to lose his balance and slip on the ladder. Sullivan grabbed his arm, stopping him from falling back to the bottom of the tunnel.

"Thanks," Connor said. "That would've sucked."

To Connor's surprise, they were standing in a large open room. There were four beds along one wall, a table with a few chairs, a TV, and a sofa. And it was clean. This room couldn't be more opposite of Diesel's home or any of the homes in the Levels. It was nicer than anything they had at headquarters, too.

"Does this TV work?" Connor asked.

"Yeah," Diesel called from a back room. "It only gets the news channel though, so it's boring."

"Is this a functioning kitchen over here?" Connor walked over to an area sectioned off with cabinets. He opened a few of the cabinets to find they were fully stocked with food. "What is this place?"

"This is my end-of-world home." Diesel tossed supplies on one of the beds and wheeled it until it was situated directly under one of the lights. "I've been stocking it for years, just in case."

"In case of what?" Sullivan asked.

"In case we start another civil war." Diesel looked at him like it was a stupid question. "I'd rather survive."

"I don't understand, Diesel." Connor turned to him, shaking his head. He never would have guessed Diesel would prepare like this. His hideout was stocked better than anything the Order had prepared. "Why live in that half-blasted home when you could live here?"

"Too isolated down here. I'd never see the sun."

"Yeah, but this place is amazing." Connor ran his fingers through his hair before he turned to a closed door on the opposite wall. He opened the door and found a clean, fully functioning bathroom.

"And I need it to stay that way." Diesel's voice was rough, irritated. "You never know what could happen."

"I suppose."

Diesel pushed past him, a change of clothes in hand, and shut the bathroom door, leaving Connor and Sullivan alone. Connor heard the shower start up, grateful that Diesel had decided to clean up before taking that thing out of Sullivan's neck.

Connor walked over to the only door that opened to the outside world and it was bolted. There were no windows to break out and the walls were made of concrete block. The only way someone from the outside was getting in was by blasting their way through. But why would they? Connor couldn't think of a reason why anyone would even look in the basement of the hospital for rebels like them. Diesel had a safe hideout, safer than anything the Order had, in the event of another war. He could come and go from the manhole cover and no one would be any wiser.

"OKAY," DIESEL SAID AS HE REJOINED them, clean and with a fresh change of clothes. "Let's get this done. Sullivan, face down on this bed."

"That was quick." Connor jerked his head around, surprised to see Diesel out so fast. He had made himself comfortable assuming Diesel would be in there a while. "Are you sure you're clean?"

Diesel didn't respond, only glared at Connor and snapped his fingers at Sullivan. Connor laughed, and Sullivan obeyed.

Once Sullivan was comfortable, Diesel peeled back the blocker patch he'd placed over it earlier and poked around his neck. A red light blinked slowly around a tiny injection wound.

"Any idea how big this thing is?" Diesel asked.

"It has to be tiny." Sullivan's voice was muffled since his head was buried in his arm. "They injected it with a needle."

"Hopefully it's not too deep." Diesel rubbed the area of his neck with his fingers, trying to feel the sensor. "Ha, found it."

"Is that a good thing?" Sullivan asked.

"Yes, it is." Diesel pressed harder on the spot where he found the chip. "Can you feel that, when I push on it?"

"Yeah," Sullivan replied, his voice strained. Connor leaned over from the opposite side of the bed and looked at the spot. He certainly hoped this would be easy. He wouldn't put anything past Dr. Hunter and feared the worst. That thing in his neck could be wrapped around nerves or veins and next to impossible to extract.

"I'm going to make this quick." Diesel reached over to his bag and pulled out a needle and a small vial. "First, a local anesthetic for the pain and then we'll get started."

"Okay," Sullivan answered. "Do what you have to do, just get that thing out of me."

Diesel injected the anesthetic in three places around the location of the chip. Connor watched him carefully as he cleaned the area and gave it a light shave before prepping his surgical tools. It wasn't that he didn't trust Diesel because he did, but he couldn't help his need to control the situation. Nothing made Connor feel worse than losing control.

Diesel ordered Connor to stand opposite the tray he set up and act as his assistant. He chuckled at how quickly Connor obeyed. Connor shot him a glare and a low growl, letting him know he shouldn't get used to this.

Diesel reached over and pressed on Sullivan's neck. "Feel that?"

"Nope," Sullivan answered.

"Great. Connor, place both hands on his shoulders, just in case." Connor stood in front of Sullivan and pressed down on his shoulders as instructed.

"Perfect. Now don't move—either of you." Diesel took the scalpel and cut a thin slit in his neck, just above where he felt the chip. He took a small clamp and spread the cut open to reveal the tendons and muscles. There was a small bit of swelling in the muscle where the device had been inserted.

"Shit." He dropped the scalpel on the tray and grabbed the anesthetic. "Looks like this thing is embedded in the muscle tissue. I'm going to give you more anesthetic."

"Is that bad?" Connor didn't like the sound of Diesel's voice. He heard worry in Diesel's tone. Connor leaned forward to see the spot Diesel was talking about. It was tiny, invisible to the untrained eye. If Diesel hadn't pointed it out, Connor never would have seen the swelling. The faint, red flashing light was the only indicator it was there.

"It makes it more painful and I don't have a lot of anesthesia. Back off some." Diesel pushed the back of his hand into Connor's chest. "You're not helping."

"I just want to make sure he's okay." Connor stood up straight, getting out of his way.

"He'll be fine," Diesel snarled.

"He better be," Connor answered with equal aggression. "His sister will kill me if I don't bring him back in one piece."

"You know, you're not as much help as I'd hoped, and he's holding still. Why don't you go watch TV or something?" Diesel gave him a nasty look before he turned back to finish the surgery.

CHAPTER NINE

2031: Day 69, Sunday

Katrina rolled over, her back aching from lying flat on the concrete floor. She blinked her eyes open and saw nothing but black. Her eyes refused to focus on anything around her. Not because her eyes wouldn't focus, but because the darkness was too thick. There was nothing to see.

She ached all over. Rubbing her neck, she tried to recall how she got here. The last thing she remembered was being trapped under a massive slab of concrete and being rescued by the handsome man who had caught her staring at him.

"Hello," she called into the darkness. No one answered her except the echo of her own voice. She slid her body up to a seated position. Every move hurt. She stretched her arms and legs out and gave them a shake. They didn't seem broken. Her chest, however, may be a different story. A searing pain shot from her left rib directly into her side. It felt like someone jabbed a dagger between her ribs and twisted.

She slowly ran her hands around her and felt a wall close

by. Her hands shook so much that her fingers skipped along the wall. Grunting with every breath, she shifted her body and positioned herself so she could lean her back against the wall and press her palms into the floor. She refused to let fear take root in her mind and keep her from getting up. The darkness overwhelmed her and the pain in her side was almost more than she could take. Letting fear creep in would be crippling. She let out a slow, deep breath and let her eyes adjust to the darkness. After a few minutes, she could see the faint lines of light along the floor where there may be a door.

Pulling her feet in close to her body, she slowly pushed herself up using the wall for support. Her legs may not be broken, but every muscle burned from the weight of her body. With one hand pressed against the wall behind her and the other pressed against her chest, she forced herself up. The explosion didn't kill her, but she felt like death.

She pulled forward to stand without the support of the wall and nearly collapsed to the floor. Quickly, she let her body fall backward until her bottom met the wall for support. Her legs were too weak to hold up her full weight and her lungs cut off her air supply. She gasped for air, panicking at her inability to breathe.

Willing herself to calm down, she remained against the wall until her breathing slowed and the pain in her chest let up. It never went away, but at least the sharp pain that made her lungs stop working reduced to a jarring throb. The longer she leaned there with her eyes open, the more she could see there wasn't anything else in this room with her. It was empty—nothing except her and the darkness.

With steady breaths, she slowly pulled her body along the wall, barely lifting her feet off the floor. Each movement took her breath away. She caught herself inspecting her ribs multiple times with her hand, searching for the knife that had to be there. She found nothing, not even an entry wound.

Her journey around the edge of the room to the doorway was the longest journey of her life. At least, it felt that way. Her fingers chafed from the constant scraping along the wall, but without it, she would have fallen. Her legs felt a little stronger than they had when she first stood, but they still trembled under her weight. Between the jabbing pain in her chest, her raw fingers and her weak legs, all she wanted to do was give up and rest. But if she stopped, even for a second, she'd never get up again. Instead, she focused on the repetition of her motions. *Breathe, step, scoot. Breathe, step, scoot,* she quietly chanted to herself, focusing only on those actions and ignoring the pain. She continued this pattern along the wall until she felt the door frame. Scooting closer, she couldn't feel a doorknob. It must be on the other side.

"Shit." She huffed out with a deep breath. Her journey wasn't over yet. She moved her foot over and paused, realizing she had no idea what would be on the other side. Scooting around the wall had taken her far longer than any walk she'd ever taken in her life. The searing pain dragged time out. In all this time, she heard no other noises except her own groans and gasps from the pain.

She waited and listened.

Nothing.

She took a deep breath and held it to quiet her lungs, but the pain was so sharp it shot through her chest and out her throat. She couldn't hold back the scream. She fell forward, her arms held out to break her fall. She curled her body into a ball and struggled to hold back the tears.

After a moment, she rolled over onto her back and let her body sink into the floor. The stillness of the weight beneath provided the slightest reprieve and her breathing slowed.

Determined to open the door, she stared at it and willed her body to respond. She dug deep, calling upon the strength of her magic to help her stand. She didn't possess any healing abilities, but the calming comfort of her magic might be enough to get her up.

All she had to do was stand.

Stand, Katrina. She controlled her body, her movements, her feelings, and her pain. Never again would someone violate her in the way that Dr. Hunter had done. Her memories of what he'd done took over her thoughts and her anger swelled, pushing the pain aside.

She pulled her feet under her once more, focused on her magic, and willed her legs to push her upright. She wobbled, but she stood, holding her ground.

All she had to do was take a step forward. Just one step, and then another. She inhaled one more deep breath and with all the strength of a roaring fire, she walked forward.

At last, her hand was on the handle and she pulled open the door.

THE LIGHT ON THE OTHER SIDE OF the door blinded her. Katrina winced at its brightness and doubled over in pain. She moved from one extreme to the next and her ribs hated her for it. She had never felt so broken in her life.

Bent over on all fours now, she took a moment to catch her breath and to let her eyes adjust to the stark contrast in light. The floor beneath her was rough, like cement mixed with gravel. It didn't take long before her hands and knees ached from the gravel digging in. She pushed herself back and rested her bottom on her feet and rubbed the pain out of her hands. Even through her jeans, the gravel beneath her cut into her knees with a fierce force.

Blinking until her eyes focused, it was clear the light

source was the sun rising over the horizon. She scanned around her, but there was nothing but open sky in front of her and the dark wall behind her. Calling upon every ounce of magic within her, she pushed her body, refusing to let herself fall over. The energy from the rising sun boosted her strength and she stood.

Katrina breathed in the fresh, cool air around her. *I will not fall. I will not fall.* Over and over again, she chanted the phrase to herself. Pushing back the pain, she took a step forward. The ground beneath her ended about twenty feet in front of her and the edge called her to continue moving forward.

Another step. Still standing.

And another.

The closer she got to the edge, the more her legs shook from weakness. She struggled to force another step forward. One more step, she told herself, one more and she'd see.

She was wrong. She took the step and saw nothing but emptiness. How could that be? She had to be somewhere. Glancing back at the door she worked so hard to get away from, she spotted a second door farther down on the right. She paused, taking the time to process her surroundings, her eyes still struggling to focus on the solid forms before her. Looking back to the edge, her blinking finally made way for clarity.

A roof. She was on a roof.

She closed her eyes to focus on the last thing she remembered. A man's face. A stranger who knew her name. He helped her remove the concrete slab off her. He picked her up and then what?

She let out a huff and wrinkled her nose. Her mind was blank. Did he bring her here? How? He would've had to carry her up from beneath the city and then up to the top of this building. That's a lot of carrying.

She slowly walked to the edge of the building, keeping her balance in check, stopping once she knew how high she was. Dropping once again to her hands and knees, she crawled to the edge. The destruction of the world below came into focus.

The Levels. How did she get this far away from the hideout? The Levels weren't exactly a hop skip and jump from where they were hiding. And to carry her this far. There had to be more than one other survivor. There was no way a single man could've done that.

Pushing herself back up to stand, grunting with every inch she moved, she turned back the way she came. She froze. Now that she was far enough away from the room she exited, she could see the skyscrapers behind her. A mix of emotions washed over her body. She was in awe at the beauty before her, especially with the sunrise glowing off the surfaces in muted yellows and oranges. What remained of Manhattan had never looked so calming and inviting.

Yet, Manhattan was a haven for the Magical Bond. A place those without magic were no longer welcome. A place she was no longer welcome. They'd long ago expelled her, the Order, and all Common Blood from that part of the city. She hated it, despised everyone and everything that remained there. But in this moment, weak and in pain, she found joy in its sight.

She glanced back towards the Levels, and she was reminded of the horror remaining after the Magical Bond bombed this portion of the city.

"That's more like it," she said to herself. Her disgust returned.

"What's more like it?" A voice called from behind.

Startled, she spun around too quickly and lost her balance. Her strength had not yet fully returned, and she fell to the ground. The gravel, mixed in with the roof's surface, cut into her hands and she yelled out in pain.

"Easy now." The man that pulled her out of the rubble gently laid a hand on her shoulder. "You okay?"

"Yeah." She brushed him off and sat back, kicking her legs out in front of her. "You startled me."

"Sorry, I didn't mean to." He sat down next to her and opened the bag he had with him. He handed her a bottle of water. "Here, you've got to be thirsty. I've got food, too."

"Thanks." She took the bottle, attempting to avoid his stare, but his soft, friendly smile pulled her eyes up to his. He had kind eyes, pale blue, almost white near the pupil. She took a drink of water to break eye contact and drank the entire bottle to keep from looking back at him. "Thank you. I needed that."

"You're welcome." Digging in his bag, he asked, "What sounds good? I've got granola bars, dried fruit, a few candy bars, and beef jerky."

"What's your name?" she asked, ignoring his question.

"Oh, yeah." He shook his head. "How dumb of me. We've never met. Name's Ajax. I'm from one of the outposts."

"Outposts?" She gave him a quizzical glance and took one of the granola bars he held out for her. She couldn't recall the last time someone from one of the outposts came to headquarters. In fact, they tried to avoid that kind of travel because it was a risk to exposure. "Which one?"

"Brooklyn North." He answered like it was no big deal, like he made that trip all the time.

"Why you?" she snapped. That didn't make any sense to her. Joanie never sent someone in her place. Ever. "Is everything okay there?"

"Oh, yeah." He waved her concern off. "Joanie had to check on some border issue we're having near the coast. She asked me to come and inform the council of the issues."

Katrina stared at him, searching for fault in his statement. In all the years she'd been a council member, Joanie had never sent someone in her place. But he did know who she was, and it was a reasonable explanation. She leaned over the edge of the building and counted six windows. She was at least six, maybe more, floors up. Looking around her, she tried to gauge how far she was from the hideout. The hideout had been at least seven blocks to the west, closer to the city center.

"How did you get me here?" she asked.

"Well," he chuckled. "I'm a lot stronger than I look. My magic gives me great strength. I can lift and carry a lot more weight for a greater distance and time than the average person. It took a while, but I got you here without notice."

"Okay." She watched his expression closely, called upon her magic to help her figure out if this man could be trusted. He left her alone and in the dark. Why had he left her where she could potentially get caught?

"I knew this place was safe," he continued. "I used to live here, before the war, before that." A sadness washed over his face when he pointed to the Levels. Katrina followed his gaze. She, too, found this view disheartening. She grew up in the Bronx. Her childhood home was flattened, and her parents murdered.

"I'm sorry about your friends." He rested his hand on her arm, drawing her attention back. His eyes captured hers. She'd never seen eyes quite like his before, the paleness of the color contrasted with his dark skin and dark hair. It was eerie, yet mesmerizing. They unnerved her, and she couldn't decide if that was good or bad.

"How long has it been?" She struggled to get back to her feet. Ajax was quick to catch her and break her fall.

"Take it easy." He provided her the strength she needed to stand up. His body was close to hers, too close. She felt his chest rise and fall with each breath he took.

"I need to get back." She pushed him away. She moved her legs too quickly and she stumbled, landing flat on her face. Her broken ribs, the pain of a twisting knife, took her breath away.

"Katrina! You need to rest." Ajax lifted her and held her in his arms. He wiped away the small drip of blood that now seeped from the fresh cut on her forehead. "You're in no shape to move yet."

"But Connor." She let out a long, slow breath. "He'll come... come... looking for me."

CHAPTER TEN

2031: Day 69, Sunday

Sullivan slept, and Connor was exhausted. It was more of a mental exhaustion, rather than physical. The surgery was over, but it had taken a lot out of all of them.

Despite the tiny size of the microchip, thin hair-like fingers protruded from one end and spread through the muscle and to the spine, weaving in with the nervous system. Dozens of fine hairs spread through his neck from this single microchip as if they had the ability to grow beyond what they were provided. It was technology unlike anything they'd ever seen.

Diesel tried to cut one of the hairs but as soon as he put the slightest bit of pressure on it, Sullivan seized up in pain. Pulling on the hairs made it worse. Sullivan screamed so loud, Connor was sure someone above heard and would break down the wall any minute.

Connor watched in horror with every scream. There was nothing he could do to make this easier on Sullivan. And to

Sullivan's credit, he endured every bit of it. He never asked Diesel to stop and he never once tried to get away. Connor wasn't so sure he would have been half as brave.

Diesel gave Sullivan the strongest painkiller he had, and it wasn't enough. He didn't have a proper drug on hand. With every move Diesel made, Sullivan screamed. He screamed until he passed out. It was only at that point that Connor was able to relax.

It was by accident that Diesel figured out how to extract it. While injecting a local anesthetic near the microchip, Diesel brushed the tip of the needle near the red flashing light and the hair-like fingers retracted, allowing Diesel to pull the chip out easily.

Sullivan seemed to be fine, at least Diesel insisted he was fine. Since the hairs retracted on their own, Diesel assumed there wouldn't be any permanent damage to his nervous system or brain function. But they wouldn't know until Sullivan woke up. Connor started to wake him, or at least try to, but Diesel stopped him.

"When can we leave?" Connor asked, checking his anger. He didn't like Diesel ordering him around.

"He needs rest." Diesel injected something into Sullivan's vein. "Lots of rest."

"What did you give him now?" Connor reached over and grabbed Diesel's arm and pulled the syringe out of his hand. It was too late.

"The last of the painkiller I have. He's gonna need more." Diesel ignored Connor's glare and rummaged through a nearby cabinet. A moment later, he smashed the microchip with a mallet. Connor watched until the red, flashing light stopped blinking.

"Is it dead?" Connor stared at the flattened microchip. It was too small to see any cracks or noticeable breaks, but it was flattened into a tiny disk and the hair-like structures frayed around the edges.

"I hope so," he answered.

Connor sighed before he turned to an empty bed and lay down. He was ready for this ordeal to be over and anxious to get back to Katrina and Charlotte. He hated leaving them behind, but he had no way of predicting how this meeting with Diesel would go. Every delay, every passing minute they waited was a risk.

The faint click of the latch made Connor shoot up in bed. Diesel was halfway down that ladder and back into the tunnel before Connor was on his feet.

"Sullivan needs more medicine and we need to get this thing as far away from us as possible." Diesel held up a small bag that contained the smashed microchip. He closed the hatch behind him and locked it into place before Connor reached the opening.

"Diesel," he screamed as loud as his voice could carry. He pulled and pulled at the hatch, but it was locked and he didn't know the combination. He and Sullivan weren't going anywhere until Diesel returned.

"You better return, asshole," Connor mumbled under his breath.

Connor paced around the room, his anger building. He was hyper-focused on each word Diesel said before that hatch closed. He said he needed more medicine for Sullivan. *Bullshit.* Connor didn't believe that for a second. He probably just needed a fix for himself. Taking the microchip with him was a smart move. He'd smashed it beyond recognition, but one couldn't be too careful where SUM was concerned. If that thing still transmitted, all of this would have been for naught.

But the sneaking out and waiting until Connor was unable to stop him or insist on doing it himself, was another reason not to trust anything Diesel said.

Connor had nothing left to do except wait.

He lay back down on the bed, exhaustion threatening to knock him over. A little sleep was all he needed, but sleep never came. All night he tossed and turned or paced the room, checking on Sullivan way more than was required. He had grown to like Sullivan over the past few months and he couldn't stand the thought of losing him, too. He'd never admit that to anyone, but his own feelings kept him constantly checking to make sure he was still breathing.

The silence of the room was maddening. Even Sullivan's breathing was barely audible. Connor had never been trapped in this much silence before in his life. He had gone from the noisy orphanage to the hustle and bustle of the city. Even his time in the wilderness involved noises. The hoot of the owls, chirp of the bugs, rustling leaves, and cracking tree branches kept him company. This room made no noises.

Hours passed, and Diesel had not returned. He had no reference for time, but it felt like days had gone by.

Connor sat down in the chair opposite the television. He stared at it, unsure of what to do. He never had a television. The community center at the Institute had been the only television he'd ever seen up close, and he never bothered to sit down and watch it. He wouldn't have known what to watch in the first place. Turning it on, he found what he thought was a news channel and left it there. He needed the noise more than the entertainment.

CONNOR SHOT OUT OF THE CHAIR WHEN a loud buzz blasted from the television. He rubbed his eyes. His exhaustion had finally taken over and he managed to sleep, though he didn't know for how long. Sullivan was still out and there was no sign of Diesel.

The buzz that woke him grew louder and transitioned from annoying to loud a shrill. He was about to turn it off when the shrill stopped and the words "Breaking News" in bright red popped up on the screen. There was a special address from the president's office. A news anchor talked for several minutes before the screen switched from the newsroom to a private office. Vivian Way stepped into view and sat down behind the desk.

"What?" Connor said. This made no sense. Why was Vivian Way giving the address, not President Finch?

"Thank you for joining me today. I wish I was coming to you today with good news. But it is with a sad heart that I must inform you we are under attack. Our government is doing everything within our power to restore peace and harmony to our great nation. The Scientific Understanding of Magic Institute, an institution sanctioned by our government, was close to a major breakthrough that would've brought us all together, Magical Bond and Common Blood alike.

"There are those who do not believe in SUM's mission, those who do not want to see magic restored to the masses. There are those who think we are trying to suppress the Common Blood. That is not what we are trying to accomplish. We are trying to understand what happened to magic. Our mission is simple, and our mission is harmless. But for reasons we do not understand, a terrorist group that calls themselves the Order of Peace, is trying to destroy our way of life.

"This group is anything but peaceful. Earlier this week, a small dispatch of rebels attacked Research Island. This attack resulted in the death of countless individuals. The attack destroyed one of our research centers, causing millions of dollars in damage, the loss of priceless data and information, and set our research back potentially by decades. These individuals also kidnapped two of SUM's most

valuable contributors. If you see these two individuals, call this number immediately."

A picture of Sullivan and Charlotte popped up on the screen with a phone number typed across the bottom.

"Their work to SUM is of most importance. If you see them, please do not approach them. Their kidnappers are dangerous and very powerful Magical Bond. They are powerful leaders of the Order. We fear interference with their plans is dangerous and they'll stop at nothing to succeed—even kill innocent bystanders."

Connor couldn't believe it. He shouldn't be surprised though. He knew better than anyone just how far SUM and this government would go to win this war.

War.

That's exactly what this meant. They were at war again. That wasn't what he or the Order wanted. He wanted to avoid a war, level the playing field so the weak could claim their place in society.

"Two days ago, we moved in on what we believe was the main headquarters for the Order of Peace. Over a hundred individuals were taken into custody, and many were killed. However, an undisclosed number of rebels escaped. We have evidence to suggest the leaders of this terrorist group escaped and are not among those we took into custody. We did not recover our key contributors. We do believe, however, they were held at this location prior to our raid.

"I'm sorry we failed to achieve our goal in capturing these dangerous individuals. They are a threat to our government and our very way of life.

"You may be wondering why I am addressing this great nation and not the President himself. Just this morning, a small group of rebels, we suspect the same ones that attacked Research Island, attacked this very office. I regret to inform you that President William Finch was assassinated during this attack. As described in the Presidential Succession Act, I have been declared the forty-eighth President of the United States of America.

"I do not step into this office with joy. These are troubled times. I've no doubt my term as your President will be rough and met with many great challenges. But I promise to do everything in my power to protect all citizens of this country and fight for a better future for both the Common Blood and Magical Bond.

"This is only the beginning and we must take drastic measures to avoid further death and destruction. Due to the dangerous nature of these individuals and their unnaturally powerful magic, I have passed my first executive order. Until these rebels are captured and are no longer a threat to society, the use of all magic is banned. Anyone caught using magic will be arrested. You and your family will be investigated for known associations with the Order and its members. We urge you to take this ban seriously. It applies to all citizens, including government and military officials. No one is exempt until these rebels are taken into custody. Violators will be prosecuted to the fullest extent of the law.

"Thank you."

Connor stared at the television long after Vivian's address was over, his eyes and ears unfocused. The news team continued to debate and analyze Vivian Way's address, but he didn't absorb anything they said.

The president was dead, and they were being blamed for it. This changed everything. In one fell swoop, Vivian exposed her plan and reasons for everything she aimed to achieve. They didn't kill the president. She did.

SUM, or rather Vivian, would pursue them until they were found. Sullivan and Charlotte would never be safe unless they permanently destroyed SUM and stopped them from doing further harm. He hoped for the latter.

Vivian risked SUM's true intentions when she exposed the events that took place at the Institute. It was a risk that had the potential to expose everything SUM had done to them and countless other individuals, both Common Blood and Magical Bond.

It was a risk he assumed she would never take.

Vivian Way did the one thing he never imagined, and now she had the upper hand.

THE STRENGTH WITHIN

EPISODE FIVE OF AFTERMATH OF DEFIANCE

CHAPTER ELEVEN

2031: Day 69 Late Sunday

Trapped beneath the city with no way to escape, Connor Vance paced the room for no reason other than to give his body something to do. His anger threatened to burst out of his skin but allowing that to happen would only make matters worse. Busting this place apart would accomplish nothing except maybe a release for his anger, a childish action he refused to allow himself to succumb to.

Sullivan's state helped to keep him in check, but only slightly. Sullivan was stable and resting. For now, that was good enough. The surgery to remove the sensor SUM installed in his neck had been more difficult than they anticipated. The pain, more than anything, forced Sullivan's body into a deep sleep. Connor hoped when he woke, he'd feel well enough to head back to the hideout where they left Katrina and Charlotte. Too much time had passed and the sounds from above worried him.

The distant booms rattling the walls left Connor uneasy

about the safety of his friends. He thought leaving them behind in the hideout would be safer than taking them on this journey with Sullivan. But the sounds left him assuming the worst about the state of the city—the city he worked so hard to save and protect. He failed in every possible way. Each bomb that dropped shook the structure around him, fueled his insecurities, and fed his anger.

But am I angry at SUM or myself? It was a question he tried to push out of his mind.

Convincing himself this wasn't his fault was an impossible task. Had he not gone to the island to kill the test subjects, a mission he couldn't fulfill after meeting them, none of this would've happened. Another truth he had to learn to accept.

He tried sleeping but no matter how exhausted he was, sleep never came. Hours had passed since Diesel ventured out through the hatch, locking it from the outside. Connor tried prying it open multiple times, but it wouldn't budge.

He stopped pacing and sat in a chair next to Sullivan's bed and listened to him breathe. The slow, steady breaths were soothing and reassuring that Sullivan would be fine. Connor focused on the rhythmic sounds hoping it would bring the much-needed sleep he needed. He felt calmer after a short sit, but sleep still never came.

The lights went out a few times, leaving them in complete darkness. The outages were short, only lasting a few minutes, but they were disorienting. The first outage was the worst. Connor wasn't prepared and had no idea where Diesel kept flashlights or candles. He bumped into every sharp corner and knocked over everything in his path as he searched. By the time the lights came back on, Connor had made quite the mess. He only had enough time to clean up after himself before the lights flickered off again. This time he waited, forced himself to focus on Sullivan's breathing until the lights were restored.

Diesel was prepared for the end of the world, a survivalist at heart. There were two small rooms beside the main open room which contained the beds and kitchen. One was the bathroom, and the second contained a large generator and a series of large tanks for a water purification system. Diesel stocked enough supplies for several people to survive down here for at least a decade without needing to search for more. By himself, he could probably live out the rest of his life with what he had. As long as he had extra fuel for the generator, Diesel could produce clean water for years. There was no way Diesel set up all this himself. The room had to predate Diesel's arrival. Most likely, Diesel knew about this room from the days he actively worked as a doctor, an advantage he had over most.

In addition to the fully stocked kitchen and crates lining the wall in the main room, the wall opposite the water purification tanks had floor to ceiling shelves at least three feet deep. Every inch of every shelf was packed with food and supplies. It was here where Connor found candles and flashlights.

Connor's worry heightened when the distant booms moved closer, shaking the walls and ceiling until it rained dust. Within minutes, the bombs fell right above them. If this room really was below Mount Sinai Hospital, that meant SUM was bombing their own kind, not just the rebel forces or those living outside the law. Connor leaned against a wall and slid to the ground. He cupped his hands over his ears to muffle the sounds of the destruction from above, an impossible task when the rumbling from the fallen rocks and stones became deafening.

A few times, Connor swore he heard screams from above. Maybe SUM had tracked them here with the sensor before it was removed from Sullivan. Why else would armed forces bomb a government-sanctioned hospital, killing their own kind, if not because of them? More reason for Connor to blame himself. He led the enemy directly to this hospital, and countless innocent people were dying above him. He tried not to think about it, but no matter how many times he told himself he had no way of knowing what was really going on above him, he assumed the worst.

Restless and unable to sleep, Connor paced the room again. This attack had to end soon. It had gone on for hours, the sounds shifting from close to far.

"Man, just sit down," Sullivan called out to him. "You're makin' me nervous."

"Hey." Connor ran to his bedside. "You're awake."

"Yeah, been watchin' you pace and it's drivin' me nuts." Sullivan sat up, wincing with each move. He stretched his neck, taking caution not to put too much strain on the cut. "Just sit and rest. You look like shit."

"I can't." A grimace covered Connor's face, causing Sullivan to shift further back onto the bed. "For all we know our friends are dead, your sister could be dead, and that asshole locked us in here."

"Your pacin' isn't helpin'." Sullivan shifted his eyes down. "And I don't need you tellin' me the danger Char could be in."

Connor brushed him off by waving his hand at him. He had no good response and nothing he said could make the situation better. "You want anything to eat? You've been out for a while."

"Food would be good." Sullivan smiled. "I'm starvin'."

"How about some soup? We have a lifetime supply of chicken noodle or chili in a can."

"Chicken noodle." Sullivan leaned his head back on his pillow and stared at the ceiling. A loud boom sounded through the room and a slight crack formed in the ceiling above him. Sullivan jerked up too fast and let out a loud yelp from the pain. "Shit."

"Take it easy. We don't have any more pain killers and with Diesel gone, don't rip out those stitches." Connor took a quick look at his bandage and didn't see any fresh blood. "You don't want me stitching them back up."

"Is that what's been keepin' you up?" Sullivan pointed in the direction of the crack.

"Yeah, it's been going on for hours." Connor walked towards the kitchen to start the soup. "It started just after Diesel left. Since I can't open the hatch, it seems we're stuck here until he returns."

"Unless that crack gets worse." Sullivan looked up at the damage from the last bomb. "It's tiny now, but a couple more direct hits and this thing could crumble down on us."

"Yeah, well." Connor followed his eyes to the same crack. "Let's not go there."

Sullivan laid back in his bed in silence until Connor returned with his soup. He slurped down several bites before he spoke again. "Worryin' will kill you, Connor. I'm sure the girls are fine."

"If you weren't in so much pain, your worry would show more too."

"Probably." Sullivan couldn't help but smile. "So, what do we do when Diesel returns?"

"I don't know." Connor rubbed his hands over his face before stretching his arms above his head. The dark circles under his eyes combined with a droopy, tired expression made him look like he aged ten years overnight. "There was a news broadcast earlier. President Finch is dead, and his assassination is being blamed on us. Vivian Way is now acting president and she's put a ban on magic."

"Geez," Sullivan said. "That sounds about right for Vivian.

She probably killed him and is usin' us to hide the murder."

"All hell broke loose up there and I've no clue what to do." Connor walked over to the television and turned it on to see if there was any news. He flipped through every channel and found nothing but white noise. With the way things sounded above, all the stations may be destroyed too. Attempting to make himself feel better, he told himself it was late into the night, and all the stations were closed.

Returning to his chair next to the bed, Connor plopped down and dropped his head into his heads. Sullivan rested his hand on his shoulder and squeezed. It was his way of letting Connor know he understood and would stick by his side no matter what happened next. They stayed like that, Connor with his head down and Sullivan staring at the crack in the ceiling, until silence fell from above.

It wasn't long before all sounds of destruction stopped. The crack remained small and unchanged, and the rattling of falling rocks ceased. Sullivan fell back asleep, which Connor supposed was a good thing. He needed Sullivan's power to be its strongest if they ever hoped to get out of here, and the more rest he got, the better. Sullivan's power of invisibility may be their best way to travel unnoticed.

At some point, Connor drifted off to sleep in the chair. The next thing he remembered was a loud bang. He jumped up out of the chair, disoriented and unsure where the noise originated. Paranoia controlled his actions, and he grabbed his gun, pointing it in front of him. There was nothing there. Sullivan remained asleep on the bed, and nothing looked out of place. He took slow, light steps towards the barred door that led to the hospital and pressed his ear against it. Nothing.

A faint click echoed from the other side of the room. Connor quickly shifted his position. Seconds later, the click was followed by the sharp squeak of the handle turning. By instinct, he dropped to his knees and steadied his aim. All rational thoughts were gone, and the only thing he cared about was keeping Sullivan safe. The hatch lid lifted, and Diesel's head popped through the opening.

"Thank God you're both okay." Diesel's voice, tired and ragged, echoed through the darkness. Connor's fury catapulted him forward. When he reached the hatch, he pulled Diesel the rest of the way through and pinned him up against the wall.

"Where have you been?" Connor yelled.

"Hey, hey, hey." Diesel's face clenched in pain. His body fell limp beneath Connor's grip. "Let me go."

"Not until you tell me what's going on and why you've been gone so long." Connor tightened his grip and pushed the gun into the side of Diesel's face.

"Put the gun down, Connor?" Diesel begged. "I'm not the enemy."

"Where have you been?" Connor leaned in closer.

"It's all-out war up there. I couldn't get back to the entrance."

"You locked us in?" The crack in Connor's voice boomed through the room and Sullivan shot up to a standing position, still half asleep. "We've been trapped down here waiting for the ceiling to collapse in on us."

"Look, man." Diesel trembled beneath his grip. "I always lock this place up. It's habit."

"That's a sorry ass excuse and you know it." Connor dropped the gun and tossed Diesel aside. Connor paced the room again, his nerves were too unhinged to stay still. "While we've been trapped in here, our friends were probably under attack. They need my help."

"Sorry. How was I supposed to know they would send out the troops?" Diesel shut the hatch and locked it. "They've destroyed everything."

Connor stopped and glared at Diesel. His heart sank as his thoughts turned to Katrina, Charlotte, and the others. Losing them and all the Order on top of Ness' and Lina's deaths was more than his mind could handle right now. "What do you mean everything?"

"There isn't a building above us for a five-block radius still standing." Diesel collapsed onto the floor next to the hatch.

Connor's anger had been in complete control and he hadn't bothered to look at Diesel or assess his condition. He was covered from head to toe with a pale, gray dust. Diesel's leg had a large gash down the side, and his pant leg was soaked through with blood. The cut was still bleeding and now a small pool of blood settled on the floor beneath him. His once quick breathing had shallowed into slow deep breaths.

"They've bombed everything. I'm lucky I made it back alive," Diesel said.

Unable to move, Connor stared at Diesel as the energy slowly drained out of him. Calmer now than when Diesel first arrived, Connor agreed—Diesel was lucky.

"What happened?" Sullivan moved as quickly as he could, which wasn't very fast, to the kitchen to get a bowl of water and some rags. Connor, still stood frozen.

"I fell from my building." Diesel's voice was faint. "My leg was trapped...under the floor...ceiling...fell...fell on top of me."

"Snap out of it." Sullivan slapped the side of Connor's arm and handed him the rags. Help me clean this wound."

Sullivan began work on cutting away the pant leg and clean the cut. It was deep and needed stitches. For now, he did his best to clean it and wrap it up until they could move Diesel to a bed. "Talk to me, Diesel. Tell me what happened."

"The bomb... they planted beneath me." Diesel's body went limp, whatever energy he had that got him here was gone.

CHAPTER TWELVE

2031: Day 69, Late Sunday

Whatever pain remained from his surgery, Sullivan pushed it aside and tended to Diesel's leg. He struggled to see the full damage of the injury. The cut was long and deep, that much he could see, but the amount of dirt and grime built up in it hid the full extent of the wound.

Sullivan rushed to the kitchen to get more water and immediately regretted his decision to run. Still weak from his own surgery, the quick movement made him dizzy, and he braced himself on the counter to keep from falling. His vision blurred, and he fumbled with every item he grabbed.

With his eyes out of focus, he splashed water all over the floor walking back to Diesel. Sitting back down helped, and within moments, his vision cleared.

Sullivan tied a long strip of fabric he cut from Diesel's pants around Diesel's thigh. It slowed the bleeding some, but not enough. Stitches were required to properly mend this wound and that was not something he nor Connor were qualified to do.

"We need to get him to the bathtub," Sullivan said. He looked up at Connor for help, but Connor only stared back in a daze. Sullivan let out a loud huff and slapped Connor on the side of his legs. "Snap out of it. Help me carry him to the bathtub."

Connor stared at Diesel's limp body. He'd made no move to help stabilize the leg or assess the full extent of his injuries. Sullivan frowned. He struggled to keep from falling over from pain and dizziness and Connor—with no injuries—was useless. There wasn't time for Connor to lose it again, and Sullivan certainly didn't have the patience for it. Sullivan hit his leg again and grunted at him.

"Sorry," was Connor's only word before scooping Diesel up and carrying him to the bathroom.

"Go find him clean cloths while I flush this out." Sullivan's voice was firm and authoritative but his body was weak. He dropped the supplies on the floor trying to sit down.

"Let me do it," Connor insisted. "You need to get back in bed."

"I've got this." Sullivan pushed him aside and leaned down to turn the water on. "Go. Clean cloths."

Connor started to object, but Sullivan glared up at him, daring him to say another word. Turning back to Diesel, Sullivan tightened the cloth around his leg once more and got to work cleaning the cut.

IT WAS SLOW WORK CLEANING UP Diesel's leg, but they finally had it cleaned, stitched, and bandaged. Every time Connor tried to help, Sullivan pushed him aside. Connor knew the reason why, and he couldn't deny he deserved the treatment. The way he froze when he realized Diesel was injured was reminiscent of how he behaved when they first arrived at headquarters. Sullivan didn't have to say anything, and even worse, Sullivan was right.

Connor immediately blamed himself for Diesel's condition, and Sullivan wasn't about to put up with another one of his self-loathing pity parties. This war was far from over and there would be many more moments just like this. They didn't have the time or energy to watch Connor spiral into oblivion over every loss. It didn't matter how it made him feel. What mattered most was how Connor responded. They needed him to be their leader, not a sympathy case. Instead of getting mad at Sullivan for rejecting his help, he tried to improve his attitude. If nothing else, that kept Sullivan from giving him another lecture.

Tending to Diesel was hard on Sullivan, but he worked through it without complaint even though every move caused him to wince from the pain. Unfortunately, antibiotics were not in Diesel's bag. Sullivan appeared safe from infection, but Diesel felt hot, and despite how well they cleaned his leg, an infection took hold. At last Sullivan found rest; his pain eased with the pain killers Diesel brought back with him.

Time blurred around Connor as he stood over Diesel watching his breathing. He focused on the moment in front of him because that was all he could control. Until Sullivan and Diesel were well and able to travel, he couldn't do anything for anyone else. But he could help them.

Diesel stirred and opened his eyes.

"How are you feeling?" Connor asked.

"Like shit." Diesel struggled to sit up in bed. He grabbed his leg and his breath caught in his chest. "What did you do?"

"You were a mess," Connor said. "We dragged your ass to the shower and flushed the cut out. It was filthy."

"Did you stitch it up?"

"Sullivan did as best he could. Neither of us was sure how to do it. We applied some antiseptic salve we found before we wrapped it, but I think you need antibiotics." Connor reached down and felt his forehead again. "You're still burning up."

"A fever is not uncommon with a procedure like this." He dropped back down on the bed. "I should be fine after a bit more rest."

"Once you can walk we need to find my sister," Sullivan called from behind them. He walked over and stopped next to Connor. "She can heal you."

"What?" He looked confused. "Is she a doctor?"

"No, she's a healer." Sullivan shrugged.

"Let me explain." Connor saw the concern on Diesel's face. He hadn't thought to prep Sullivan on how to address their enhanced powers with Common Blood. The tone of Sullivan's voice indicated Diesel should know what he meant by her being a healer. "Sully and his sister a possess special magic, somewhat like me, yet different."

"They can control me with their mind?" Diesel shifted his stare from Sullivan to Connor.

"No, their powers are different than mine but equally unique."

"What makes you unique?" Diesel turned his head back to Sullivan waiting for an answer.

"I can make myself invisible." Sullivan smiled.

"Bullshit!" Diesel coughed. He was too weak for this level of excitement.

Sullivan smiled and his body faded out of view. "I can make you disappear with me, too."

Diesel's cough worsened and he retreated backward,

almost falling off the edge of the bed at the sound of Sullivan's voice in the thin air. Connor grabbed his arm, pulling him back to the center of the bed.

A hand touched Diesel's leg where a hand couldn't be. "What the hell." Diesel's body trembled under the invisible touch. His body disappeared just like Sullivan's had done.

The hand lifted, and Diesel immediately came back into view. Sullivan, however, remained invisible. Terror consumed Diesel's face when Connor disappeared, too.

"Stop it," Diesel yelled.

"That's enough, Sully." Connor pulled his arm away from Sullivan, breaking the magic making him invisible. "You're freaking Diesel out. We still need his help to get out of here."

"Sorry," Sullivan said, letting his own body materialize.

"How can you do that?" Diesel's voice shook, and his nerves heightened. His body still trembled, but his face looked a bit calmer.

Connor pulled up a chair and sat next to the bed. He looked at Diesel, carefully considering how to proceed. He knew he needed to tell him the truth, but also knew Diesel wouldn't easily accept it. He couldn't afford to push Diesel away because he needed his help. For one, getting out of here would be a lot easier with Diesel. One wrong turn through one of those tunnels could get one or both of them killed. Plus, having a trained doctor was a valuable resource they may need again.

"I'm not really sure where to start with this," Connor said.

"Just tell him the truth, man." Sullivan laid back down on his bed. "Wake me when you're ready to go."

"What haven't you told me, Connor?" All the fear drained out of Diesel's face. He now looked at Connor with concern that could easily turn to anger.

"Keep in mind, you and I, we're on the same side no matter what SUM has done."

"Just get to the point, Connor."

"Okay." Connor took a deep breath. "SUM has been experimenting with Magical Bond and has figured out how to enhance magic during fetal development. It's not an accident that I have special powers others do not." Connor watched Diesel closely, expecting some kind of response, but Diesel stared with a blank expression.

"Go on," Diesel said after the long pause.

"Turns out I was created by SUM."

"What do you mean created?" Diesel shifted his arms underneath his sides for support. If he could move, he looked like he would've bolted out the bed.

"How do I explain this?" Connor looked to Sullivan. He'd already curled back up in bed and had his eyes closed. Whether he was asleep or not didn't matter. Connor wasn't going to get any help from him. "I wasn't born the old fashion way. I was created in a petri dish."

Connor paused again, watching Diesel's reaction. His expression was steady, intent. Connor continued before Diesel could ask any questions. "During fetal development, SUM did something to our cells. I'm not sure how, but they enhanced our magical cells during the early stages of development."

"But I thought you were raised in an orphanage upstate?" Diesel shook his head.

"I was." Connor relaxed now that Diesel seemed more relaxed. "They placed me there."

"Why would they do that?" Diesel tucked a pillow below his back to help him sit up straighter and stretched his leg out. He started to unwrap his bandages.

"Is that such a good idea?" Connor reached his hand out

and stopped Diesel.

"Yeah, I need to check the stitches. Blood is seeping through the bandage." He pushed Connor's hand away and continued unwrapping the bandage. "I need to look for signs of infection, too. Hand me my bag over there."

Connor picked up the bag and continued his story. "Anyway, it was one big experiment SUM planned from the get-go. Genetically modify a person's magical ability in vitro, expose them to drastically different emotional environments, and study the effects these emotional drivers have on their ability to use their enhanced magic. Turns out my life was planned to be an emotional disaster."

"You do realize that makes no sense."

"I do." Connor rubbed his hand over his mouth, stifling a laugh. "Unfortunately, sense has nothing to do with it. There isn't much SUM has done that makes sense to me."

"And Sully, he's enhanced too?" Diesel glanced over at Sullivan who was snoring.

"Yep, and his sister. There are a couple others as well, all with different special powers."

"I take it this means you're the reason for the current attack that wiped out everything above us?" Diesel placed a wooden rod in his mouth and bit down before he put pressure on his cut. Blood gushed out from a few areas where the stitches weren't pulling the skin together. Diesel motioned for Connor to pick up the staple gun next to his leg. Diesel mumbled a few sounds, but Connor couldn't make out the words.

"Wait." Connor shook his head. "You want me to staple your leg?"

Diesel nodded.

Connor hesitated before he stepped forward and pinched

the skin between the staple gun. He closed his eyes and pulled the trigger. Diesel let out a muffled scream and motioned him to continue. Three stables later, the open sections of his wound were closed. He took the rod out of his mouth, panting.

"Water...please." Diesel fell back on the bed.

Connor ran to the kitchen and returned seconds later. Diesel pulled himself back up and downed the glass of water. Taking a few deep breaths, he wrapped clean bandages around his wound. Connor was amazed anyone could handle that much pain without a stronger anesthetic. He wasn't sure he could do it with such calmness and saw Diesel in a whole new light now.

"So." Diesel let out a deep sigh. "We have you to thank for the bombing."

"Probably, to some degree." Connor focused on the empty space in front of him. He sat back in his chair and watched Diesel closely. He knew better than anyone how crazy he sounded. Even he struggled to grasp the truth, and he lived it.

"As a doctor," Diesel looked at him with trusting eyes, "I get the enhancement. I understand how that could work and the desire to do it. But something tells me there's a lot more you have to say."

"Well, yeah. That's the abridged version. It's a much longer story, actually."

"I'm all ears." Diesel waited for him to respond.

Connor told him everything—about the mission, and how they planned to kill the enhanced. About the first fight with the council, the one he disobeyed because they didn't agree with killing them. He told him how he and the others infiltrated Research Island. How he met Sullivan and his sister, Charlotte. He told him how Ness and Lina died along with Maggy and her endless well of magic. Telling him about Ebony, about how she saved them and sacrificed herself so they could escape was the hardest. Connor told Diesel everything about Dr. Hunter's plans and why he was doing what he did. He left no detail out.

Diesel didn't say a word while Connor spoke. He let Connor go through every event in painstaking detail. Even after Connor finished his story, he remained silent. Connor couldn't even rely on the sounds from above to break up the tension, not anymore. The bombings had stopped.

"So," Diesel said, finally breaking the silence, "nothing is certain anymore except death."

"Well." Connor laughed. It felt good to laugh, even a little. "I would still like to avoid death if that's okay with you. At least for a bit longer. And when you're up to it, I'd appreciate it if you would lead us out of here."

"Even if I agreed, there's no way we can get out of here unseen."

Connor's grin grew and he glanced back towards Sullivan. He looked back to Diesel, raised his eyebrows, and shrugged his shoulders.

"You can't be serious?" Diesel looked at him like he was crazy. "Can he make us both invisible?"

"Yeah, no one would see us coming."

"Well, we won't be leaving today. Maybe tomorrow but not likely." Diesel adjusted in his bead and prepared for a long nap. "I need to let this wound heal before I try to walk. This could take a while."

"Fine, so long as we get out of here. Rest today and we'll see how it looks tomorrow. If you're up to it, maybe you can try walking."

Connor handed him some painkillers and more water before he settled back in bed. Before he knew it, Diesel was out cold and snoring out of tune with Sullivan. Connor curled up in his bed and pulled the blanket up to his neck. He hadn't realized how chilly it was until he laid down. The exhaustion had finally won, and Connor's eye barely had time to close before he was sound asleep.

Chapter Thirteen

2031: Day 70, Monday

An unfamiliar weight pushed down on Katrina's chest. She blinked several times, letting her eyes adjust to the early morning light. A soft, warm breath tickled the back of her neck. Glancing over her shoulder, Ajax slept next to her with one arm wrapped over her waist.

The closeness of this stranger and the ease at which she allowed herself to curl up next to his body surprised her. She knew nothing about him and yet she sensed trust and safety in his presence. She gently lifted his arm, trying not to wake him, and slid her body away from his. Glancing around her surroundings, they remained in the same rooftop room she woke to yesterday. At least she thought that was yesterday. Her sense of time was distorted, and she was unsure how long it had been since the explosion killed most of the people she knew.

She didn't want to think about those deaths anymore or Charlotte, but her recent memories haunted her. It sickened her to think about what Dr. Hunter could be doing to Charlotte now that he had her back. The memories of what he did to her, the invasion of her mind and body, threatened to consume her thoughts daily, and she had to actively force them away. Now she had more death and the loss of Charlotte to accompany those memories, which further threatened to cripple her. Katrina glanced at Ajax and focused on his breathing. Even sleeping, covered in dirt and grime, he was handsome.

She pushed the negative memories aside and searched her mind for how she came to be curled up next to Ajax like this, but she drew a blank. The last thing she remembered was telling him she had to get back. Connor would come looking for her. If she wasn't there, he would panic when he saw the destruction and assume the worst.

Standing was much easier this morning than the last time she tried. Her chest still hurt, but a stinging jab didn't shoot through her with every breath she took. Katrina stretched her arms above her head and took in a deep breath of cool air. The air caught in her lungs a little because of the pain, but it was bearable. The morning breeze was crisp and now that she had pulled away from Ajax's body heat, she shivered. All they had to keep warm were the clothes on their backs, and her clothes were flimsy and torn.

"You're up," Ajax's voice called from behind her. "How do you feel?"

"Better." She turned to face him and watched him push himself up to stand. His snug, short sleeve shirt revealed the defined lines of his biceps and chest. His shoulders were broader than she recalled, but then again, her last good view of him was in the darkness of the hideout just before it blew. She shifted her eyes to his face, and he was smiling at her. Embarrassed, she turned to face the opposite direction. "My head hurts, but at least I can breathe without keeling over in pain."

"You should still take it easy. Rest more before you try to move too much." He pulled a water bottle out of his bag and handed it to her.

Exhausted and disoriented, she hadn't realized how thirsty she was. She took it and drank half of it in one gulp.

"You need to eat more too. You haven't had much in the past two days," Ajax said.

She started to refuse the apple he offered her, but the loud growl of her stomach caused him to raise his brows. She was starving and adding the water to her empty stomach only reminded her just how hungry she really was.

"Thanks." She took the apple and the granola bar he handed her. "Is that how long I've been out? Two days?"

"No, you woke briefly yesterday, but I'd say you got a good twelve hours sleep." His smile remained, charming and uncomfortable.

She wasn't used to people smiling at her like that, whatever *that* was. She wrapped her arms around herself and rubbed her arms.

"Sorry, I tried searching for blankets yesterday, but I couldn't find any close. We'll have to search for supplies today. Stock up," he said.

"How much food do we have?" She looked at the apple she already half ate and felt the guilt.

"A few days' worth if we ration what we have. But you need to heal, and I don't want to limit your food intake by much." He glanced up at her with a look in his eyes she didn't understand. A rush of warmth washed over her face, and she turned away for fear her cheeks were blushing. She took a quick loop around the room. The only difference from yesterday was the window was now uncovered to let in the sunlight.

She turned back to Ajax who counted the granola bars as he laid them out in front of him. They had a good amount and could probably make it last a week if necessary. Ajax had two unopened boxes of granola bars, a large bag of dried fruit, two more apples, and a few packs of beef jerky. The jerky alone could get them through Wednesday as long as they had plenty of water.

"There's a convenience store not too far from here, or at least there was one. We can check there for more supplies before we head out," Ajax said.

"Let's get moving then." She took the last bite of the apple and smiled as the sweet juice filled her mouth. Funny how two days without a real meal can make something as simple as an apple feel like a dream. "Best to travel early."

"We should stay here for at least one more day. Check the store and come back here."

"No," she said, too quickly. "I've already been gone too long."

"Katrina, no one is there." His facial expression turned grave, and all the charm drained away. "They're either dead or taken by SUM. Nothing good can come of going back."

"I have to go back. Connor may have already returned. He needs to know I'm fine." She turned towards the stairway, but Ajax grabbed her arm.

"It's not safe." He pulled her close to his body. So close, she could feel the movement of his chest against her own. "SUM is looking for you. If you go back now, they'll capture you, too."

"I can't stay here, I have to find Connor." She pulled away, regaining some distance between them. Her movement had been too quick though, and the pain of her broken ribs jabbed her lungs. Her breathing quickened, and her chest tightened. The pain put too much pressure on her lungs, making it difficult to breathe. Being that close to him only made it worse. "You don't have to go. Stay here where you're safe. I can't ask you to risk your life for us anyway."

"Are you crazy?" He picked up his bag, repacked with all their supplies and rested his hand on her shoulder. "After all I went through to get you out of there safely, we're in this together now. If you're hell-bent on going back, you're not going alone." He smiled and walked over to the stairway door. Holding it open, he waved for her to follow. His pale blue eyes and comforting smile won her over. Even her magic nudged her to follow him. Still, she remained planted where she stood surprised by his willingness to help her.

"Well, let's do this," he said after she still didn't move towards the door. "You're right about one thing. Getting an early start is the safest bet."

She stepped up to the door and he handed her a flashlight. Her fingers lightly brushed over his when she took it from him, and a wave of excitement rushed through her body. Her cheeks flushed when the grin on his face grew. She tugged at her magic, but it resisted her pull. A man had never made her feel quite like this, and she didn't know what to do with it. *Is this attraction?* She couldn't tell, and her magic was useless at the moment.

The only man she'd ever remotely been attracted to was Connor and one kiss from him was all it took to know it wasn't real. Their attraction had been brotherly and sisterly, nothing more. There had never been anything physical between them. Since that kiss, their relationship grew into a bond stronger than any romance could have created. They were family, and she needed to find him.

She pushed the confusing thoughts about Ajax to the back of her mind and continued to play tug-of-war with her magic. She wanted a protective barrier around her, but her magic wanted her to open up to Ajax. At least her magic trusted him. It more than trusted him—it was trying to pull them closer together. She thought she knew everything her magic could do, but this pull was new. She liked to think she was more in tune with her magic than anyone else, she understood its mystical powers as well as it's protective powers. But this magical behavior was different than anything she'd experienced. Her magic had never disobeyed her before, and this time it did.

She was three steps into their descent down the stairway when the door behind them slammed shut. She drew in a breath. She looked back at Ajax, unable to hide her surprise.

"Sorry." He shrugged.

"It's okay. It was just loud and unexpected." She turned forward and shined the flashlight in front of her, lighting the steps. "How far down?"

"Six stories, I think."

She cringed at the thought of walking down six stories. Her chest may feel better than yesterday, but each step jabbed at her broken ribs. Walking on a flat surface wasn't so bad, but downward was a different story. It was going to be a slow walk.

It took forty-five minutes, four long stops, and countless extremely slow downward steps before they emerged from the first-floor door and into the abandoned foyer of the apartment building. Katrina was out of breath, her legs weak and wobbly, while Ajax looked like he exerted no effort at all.

"Well, that was harder than I expected." Katrina grinned and slid down the wall to sit on the floor. She took a sip of water, her bottle almost empty. "How much water do we have?"

"Maybe a half dozen bottles." He dug around in his bag. "Seven. Here, give me yours. I'll check for running water."

She handed him her bottle and he disappeared around

the corner. Aside from his footsteps walking away, there were no other sounds. This building was empty. From where she sat, she could see out the front window. The sun was full in the sky, and everything outside looked gray, covered in dirt and rubble. Whatever happened out there looked bad. She pushed herself up to her feet, gasping when she pulled her legs underneath her and stood. The pain from yesterday had returned and it nearly knocked the air out of her chest. Pressing her hand to her side, she felt her ribs and found the break. With the tips of her fingers, she gently pressed each rib, fighting back the scream. Three breaks. No wonder it felt like someone jabbed her with a knife and continuously twisted it.

"No more steps today," she whispered to herself. She slowly made her way to the window to look at the conditions outside. "Please don't let there be steps out of the building." Resting her hand on the glass, she leaned forward and smiled. No more steps, but the ground was covered in rock and large debris. She tried not to think about how hard walking that terrain would be with broken ribs. One step at a time. All she had to do first was make it to the convenience store.

"Good news," Ajax said, walking up behind her. "Plenty of water. I found a few more bottles to fill as well. How you feeling?"

"Terrible." She smiled as she took her water bottle back, downing another drink. "How far is that convenience store?"

"Not far. To the right a couple blocks or so."

"Let's start by making it there," she said. "See what we find."

"Okay." He took her arm, offering her support. "You ready?"

"Ready as I'll ever be." She smiled and wrapped her arm around his shoulder, letting him carry the bulk of her weight.

If she had any hope of making it back to Connor, she'd have to rely on Ajax for help. And lots of it.

CHAPTER FOURTEEN

2031: Day 70, Monday

They made it half a block before Katrina stopped. The thought of taking another step brought tears to her eyes. The amount of rock and debris in their path was more of an obstacle than either of them predicted. The only way through it was climbing over it, and that caused Katrina more pain than any other movement.

"Maybe I should go the rest of the way alone?" Ajax said, helping her slide down to a seated position.

"No, I can make it." Katrina refused to give up and let her injuries keep her down. Wiping her face dry to hide the tears, she pushed herself up straight. Rest was what she needed, but rest would have to wait a little longer. Now was the time to push through, not cower back in pain. "I'll be fine if we can find a route that requires less climbing. What if we walk closer to the buildings over there? Looks like it could be a clearer path."

"We can try, might take longer," Ajax said.

"Longer is fine as long as reduces the strain on my chest." She took a deep breath and pressed her hand on her broken ribs. The slight pressure provided a moment of relief. A bandage to wrap around her would minimize movement and provide the constant pressure she needed to hold her ribs in place. All she had to do was make it to the store Ajax was leading her to and find it still standing. *Please let it still be standing.* If it wasn't, they'd have to find an alternative way to bandage her chest.

"You rest a moment and let me check out that path, see if I can find a clearer route before we move on." Ajax slid his backpack off and put it next to her. He leaned down and kissed her on the top of her head before disappearing around the large rock she was hidden behind.

What was that? Her body involuntarily twitched at his kiss. She hadn't expected that, though there was no denying an attraction between them. She caught him staring at her more than he caught her staring at him. They shared moments of comforting smiles regularly, but a kiss, that seemed like a jump to her. Granted it was on top of her filthy head, but a significant jump, nonetheless.

The real question she needed to answer was how she felt about it. Her body's reaction had been out of surprise, not dislike. She pulled her knees in close to her and dropped her head down to think this through. Truth be told, she daydreamed about what it would be like to kiss him on the lips more than once this morning. She'd never been in a relationship before, at least not a real, adult relationship, and she was unsure how to act. She was even more unsure of what was normal. For all she knew, kissing someone you're attracted to on top of the head was normal.

The uncertainty made it impossible for her to act on her feelings. *Feelings?* She wasn't even sure if she was willing to say she was developing feelings for Ajax. An attraction didn't mean feelings, it just meant she thought he was good to look at. *Right?*

"Come on, dummy," Katrina mumbled under her breath. "Get a grip." There were so many more important things to be thinking about right now. The last thing she needed to do was get involved with a guy she hardly knew. *Find Connor, rescue friends.* That's the focus, not Ajax and his well-defined muscles.

"Get a grip on what?" Ajax said as he sat down next to her.

His voice startled her, and she jerked her head up too quickly. The pain in her chest jabbed her lungs.

"Sorry, didn't mean to startle you."

"No, just didn't hear you walk back." She readjusted, putting a bit more distance between them. She dropped her head on her knees to hide her red face. "I'm just worried about my friends. Does that way look easier to walk?"

"I think so." He opened his bag and took out his water bottle. "There may be a couple areas you have to climb, but not many. Whenever you're ready, we'll give it a go."

"I'm ready." Katrina pushed herself up, fighting back a groan. She held one hand steady on the wall behind her, and the extra support relieved some of the pressure. "If we could find something I could use as a walking stick, that might help, too."

"How about a piece of rebar from the rubble?" Ajax dug around the remains of the fallen buildings until he found a piece that was short enough to work. "Here, try this. And if we come across any trouble, it makes a great weapon."

Katrina smiled and took the rebar. She took a couple steps and found it helped quite a bit to reduce the pressure on her ribs. "This will work."

Ajax nodded and motioned for her to follow him around

the corner. Moving again was good. Despite the pain, walking at least distracted her mind because she had to focus on where she placed her feet. Besides, there would be plenty of time to figure out Ajax and what he meant to her, but after she found Connor and this war ended.

KATRINA STARED AT THE BANDAGES, unsure of which wrap would ease her pain the most. She'd never been very good at caring for injuries, especially her own. Growing up, she rarely had accidents that resulted in injuries like this, and she was out of her comfort zone with what to do.

One thing she knew for certain, putting pressure on her broken ribs reduced her pain. She felt that relief when she used her hand to brace her injury. One of these tight wraps seemed like just the thing to do that, and all she had to do was pick one.

She didn't expect so many choices. The store was untouched by scavengers and somehow managed to survive all the explosions. One wall was damaged, but overall it was in great shape considering the surroundings. They had their pick of supplies.

Forcing herself to make a decision, she grabbed a bandage that would wrap around her midsection several times and filled a bag with as many bandages as it would hold. Having back up options was a good idea.

While she was at it, she cleared the shelves of all the band-aids, ointment, and pain killers they had stocked. Who knew what the next several days had in store for them? Supplies like this could be a lifesaver.

Katrina walked towards the back of the store, taking other supplies and food she wanted, leaving plenty behind for others that might wander upon this store and need food.

At the end of one of the isles, she found a rack of backpacks and transferred most of her supplies to one. She grabbed a couple extras just in case. Her hands were full and the bags were heavy. Before grabbing more supplies, she headed to the back of the store to find a private location to wrap her chest.

"Jackpot!" When she rounded the last aisle, she stopped and smiled. This store had a pharmacy. She didn't know what would be helpful, but stronger pain killers and antibiotics were definitely on the agenda. Most of the labels meant nothing to her, but the shelves were labeled with general titles of the types of drugs contained on each shelf. It didn't take her long to find the right shelf and pack more supplies in her now overweight bags. She took everything that would fit, even the ones she wasn't sure about. She may not know much about this stuff, but someone else might.

"Hey." Ajax stood next to her holding several weighted bags. "You found the good stuff and some backpacks. Were there more of those?"

"Yeah, end of that last isle there. I figured some stronger pain killers could help." She forced a smile.

"Be careful with some of those. They can make you groggy."

"You know about these?" Katrina held a few bottles out for Ajax. "Never had a need for medicine, so I don't know one from the other."

"Yeah, my mom was a nurse." He looked through the bottles she had already pulled until he found one that was suitable for her. "This one. It's not as strong as some of the others but it shouldn't make you sleepy. It'll relieve the pain enough to keep you moving. You can take a stronger one when we stop for the night if you need it."

"Thanks." She swallowed one pill and put the rest in the backpack she packed with her personal supplies. She pulled out the bandage she chose and handed it to Ajax. "Do you mind helping me wrap up my ribs? I found these bandages that might help limit movement."

"Sure, great idea." He took the bandages from her and pointed to the desk along the back wall. "Let's move back here where you can sit."

Katrina followed him to the desk and sat down. A rush of relief washed through her as the desk absorbed the weight of her body, giving her legs a break. It took a lot out of her to walk this far and more than just her ribs were screaming at her for the effort. Her legs had no visible injuries, but they hurt all the same. She watched Ajax pull out the different wraps and compare them.

"This one looks good. It should hold it tight enough to limit movement." He placed one next to her and put the others back in the bag. It wasn't the one she settled on, but she didn't care. "Okay, take your shirt off."

She crossed her arms around her chest and retreated back towards the wall. She knew her shirt had to come off before she asked him to help her, but the bluntness of his words surprised her.

"How else am I going to get this done?" He smiled. "Don't worry, I won't look."

"Yeah, right." She clenched the hem of her shirt with both hands and pulled it up over her head. A shiver ran through her body, her nakedness bringing on a chill. For once, she was grateful she slept with her bra on the night of the explosion. The grimace on Ajax's face confirmed he wasn't looking at her breasts, but rather the large purple and black bruise covering her entire midsection. "Does it look that bad?"

"Actually, yeah." He glanced up at her face and held her stare. "It looks a lot worse than it did yesterday. I shouldn't have let you move so soon."

"You couldn't stop me no matter what you tried or said." She leaned to the side to get a better look at her injury. "It would've looked like this even if we stayed."

"I suppose." He let out a low huff and picked up the bandage. "Hold your arms up over your head."

She winced as she lifted her arms. Her ribs already hurt like hell and holding her arms up only made it worse. She took a deep breath and held it when Ajax placed his hand on her side. His touch was warm, yet it sent a shiver down her spine. He leaned in close to her side, so close she could feel his breath brush against her skin. If she wasn't already holding her breath, this certainly would've taken her breath away. As it was, she had to remind herself to breathe, but breathing hurt so much worse with her arms up.

"I'm sorry." Ajax looked into her eyes, concern covering his face. "I'm almost done."

Katrina nodded and wrinkled her nose, her eyes closed tight. Her body tugged in two directions. The pain pulled her away from his touch, screaming at him to stop, and an attraction she could no longer hide from begged him to touch her more. Allowing herself to glance down at his face, a kindness settled in his eyes, one she hadn't noticed before. *Did he feel this too?* What would happen if he moved his hands a little further up? Or if she dropped her arms and wrapped them around his neck?

Stop it. She didn't have time to think about such things. All that mattered right now was patching herself up enough to make it back to the hideout and find Connor. This selfish desire had to wait.

"There." Ajax stood back and smiled. "Hopefully that helps."

Katrina dropped her head, certain her cheeks were flushed. She fumbled to pick up her shirt and straighten it out. *How did such a simple task become so difficult?* It took her way too long to slip it overhead and once she was done, Ajax was still staring at her. His smile grew when their eyes met.

"What?" she asked.

"Nothing." He shook his head. "It's just." He paused and looked to the floor. He grabbed his backpack and busied himself with repacking the supplies.

"It's just, what?" She pressed further. She combed her fingers through her long blonde hair, doing her best to make it look decent. Braiding it to hide its tangled mess would make her feel better, but she needed a hair tie to hold it in place. She sensed his attraction and wanted him to say what was on his mind, if for no other reason than to ease her own feelings and make it real. She leaned in his direction, hoping that would be enough of a signal to get him to talk.

He lifted his hand and brushed it over her cheek. "You're beautiful."

He turned away and headed towards the front before she could respond to his words. In a way, she was glad he left her so he wouldn't see the smile that took over her face, but she would've rather he stayed and acted on his desires. Sliding off the desk, she picked up one of the bags she had overstuffed with supplies. The weight of it forced an involuntary grunt. Hearing her grunt, Ajax rushed to her side. He reached for the bag but grabbed her hand instead. This time they both flushed.

"I'll carry the heavy ones. You stick to a light backpack." He put the bag down and handed her a jacket. "Found these up front. Figured we could both use one."

"Thanks. If we're going to make it, I have to be able to carry some of this stuff. This is too much for you to carry." She pulled the bag back and set it on the desk.

"You've got three there, and I've got one. Let's see about

repacking some of this to condense it down." She felt Ajax's eyes on her. He placed his bag down next to hers and smiled. Her magic sensed his desire to move in closer to her. If she hadn't turned away when she did, he would've kissed her. As much as she desired to feel his lips connected with hers, she wasn't ready for that.

At least not yet.

CHAPTER FIFTEEN

2031: Day 72, Wednesday

The sun was shining bright and the wind was fierce. A little boy stood on the hillside, fighting to stay standing. He was much younger and smaller than the other kids who were able to keep their feet planted firmly on the ground. Only their hair and clothes were tossed around by the relentless wind.

But not for him.

His feet bounced forward and backward, depending on the direction of the wind. He tried flying one of the kites, but the wind was too strong for his little body to control it. After a few of the older kids pushed him, helping the wind knock him over flat on his face, he gave up and laid down on his back on the hillside. He may be too small to fly the kites in this wind, but he could see every one of them, maybe better than if he remained standing.

There were too many kites in the air to count. Someone could, he was sure of that, but not him. He didn't know how to count past ten, so he counted ten over and over again.

It wasn't the number of kites that caught his attention, but rather the bright colors in the sky. Some were more beautiful than any work of art he'd ever seen, gold and red dragons with long, flowing tails or vivid, blue butterflies with ribbons swirling around. There was one that looked like a house. The most colorful house ever made. It was long and rectangular, mostly orange with shiny, gold trimmings. When the gold trimmings caught the sun just right, they forced his eyes to blink. The long ribbons that flowed from it looked like flames chasing it in the wind. When the sun caught the reflection of the flames just right, they danced like real fire. He didn't know why anyone would want a burning house, but it was beautiful, nonetheless.

Only six of the kites in the air belonged to his friends. Theirs were the simplest kites in the sky—single colored diamond shapes with one short ribbon to trail in the wind. His friends didn't care that they were simple and plain. These rare occasions of fun outweighed any jealousy over the extravagant kites of the other kids. The joy of being able to look upon the other kites was a rare joy. He and his friends were going to enjoy themselves no matter how plain their kites were in comparison.

They weren't really his friends, and they weren't very nice to him, but he called them friends anyway. He didn't care that he got in trouble a lot because of their pranks, and he didn't mind the trouble so long as they let him hang around. He needed them because they were the closest things to friends he had. It was them or no one.

Lying on the ground, watching the kites, was the happiest he'd ever been. It was festival day, and this was his first attendance. He didn't understand what festival day was, but he saw the happiness on the faces of others and he felt it in the air. Festival day meant they got to fly kites and eat ice cream. It meant they got to drink sodas and play games. All things they never got to do at the orphanage.

Happy.

Everyone was happy.

Even the older kids were too happy to pick on him much more, like the fun shoving they did to knock him over in the wind. They were too happy to care and too happy to notice he enjoyed lying on the ground watching the kites dip and dive in the sky.

"Connor. Hey, Connor." He turned his head towards the sound of someone calling his name, but no one was there. He turned back towards the sky to watch the kites, but they were gone. The wind had died, and the sky turned a pale, cloudy gray.

"Connor get up. Connor." The voiced called his name again. He looked around, but he was alone on the grassy hillside, all his friends and all the other kids flying kites had vanished. He stood to look over the hill's crest, but his vision faded, and his body was surrounded by dense fog. He closed his eyes and rubbed them hard. When he opened them again, he was staring at Sullivan.

"Geez, you were out cold." Sullivan stood up. "Glad you got some sleep."

Connor sat up, blinking his eyes to adjust to the light. He stretched his hands above his head and yawned. His neck cracked, and his back was stiff. Being brought back to reality made him wish he could go back to the dream. The day at the festival was one of the few happy memories he had. Until now, he'd forgotten all about that day flying kites. As he sat in the darkness of a hidden bunker, the memory was all he could think about. The joy and relaxation of that moment was his driving force, the dream he wanted for everyone, Magical Bond and Common Blood alike.

"How long have I been out?" Connor dropped his head into his hands and rubbed his eyes.

"A while, you missed lunch and dinner," Sullivan said. "Diesel is in the bathroom cleanin' up. I think he's feelin' a little better. He's walkin' at least."

"Good." Connor stood and stretched out his back. "We've been here too long."

"It's only been a couple days, Connor." Sullivan handed him a cup of coffee. "We all needed the rest, you just as much as us. I dug around his supplies and found him a walkin' stick he can lean on. Without that, I don't think we'd get very far. Even with it, I think we're goin' to be carryin' him most the way."

"As long as we can get out of here and he's willing to help." Connor's stomach growled. He hadn't eaten since yesterday.

"I made dinner," Sullivan said, hearing Connor's stomach. "Go eat. It might be the last cooked meal you have in a while."

In the kitchen, Connor found a pot of spaghetti and a tray garlic bread. A simple meal, but it smelled delicious. He piled twice as much pasta onto the plate than he would usually eat and lathered it in sauce. Diesel even had Parmesan cheese. Parmesan was rare and expensive these days. It had become one of those luxury items one only pulled out on special occasions. He sprinkled so much on his plate he could hardly see the red sauce beneath it.

Connor stood over the counter and shoveled food in his mouth. Once he took the first bite, he couldn't stop eating. He hadn't eaten much in the past couple days, and his stomach kept screaming for more.

"Feel better?" Sullivan asked. "Did you even taste it?"

"Man, I'm hungry." Connor wiped his face and refilled his plate. He turned to sit back down in his chair when Diesel walked out of the bathroom. "Thanks, Diesel. This was good."

Diesel nodded and lifted his leg up onto the bed. He laid a towel under his leg and started unwrapping his bandage.

"How's it feeling?" Connor asked.

"It aches, but no more than expected." Diesel winced when he lifted the last bit of bandage off and a fresh trickle of blood seeped from one end. After inspecting his stitches, he put more ointment on it and taped on a fresh bandaged. "I don't see any signs of an infection, at least."

"When do you think we can head out? I'd like to get back to my friends, make sure they're okay."

"Tonight, I think," Diesel said. "I can walk fine. Slow, but fine. Best to use the cover of darkness to our advantage."

"That's probably wise." Connor downed a glass of water. "Who knows what we'll find when we get out of the tunnel."

"Take a shower and get some more rest. Sullivan already packed supplies." Diesel pointed towards the hatch leading to the tunnel. Three fully packed backpacks sat next to it. "We'll leave well before dawn."

"Looks like you guys have it under control." Connor finished eating and cleaned his dishes before he took a quick shower. Diesel had even put out clean clothes for him to wear. He was almost as grateful for the clean clothes as he was for the food. He hated the feeling of dirty clothes on a clean body. It reminded him of his younger days living in the woods of upstate New York.

He curled up in bed and was asleep the moment he closed his eyes.

CONNOR CHECKED THE SUPPLIES SULLIVAN packed

earlier to make sure they had everything they'd need. He had no clue how long it would take them to reach the hideout, and they had to be prepared for anything.

Diesel woke before the others and was wrapping a couple of boards that extended above his knee tight against his leg. Connor was confused at first but quickly saw the genius in Diesel's plan. The boards made a great makeshift cast to stabilize his leg. With his stiff leg and the walking stick, he was able to walk well enough and reduce the pain from the weight of his body. With a little luck, Connor and Sullivan wouldn't have to be his support, and they'd be able to move more quickly.

"We ready?" Connor looked at both of them standing with their backpacks on. "So, how do we get you down that ladder?"

"One of you should go down first," Diesel said. He sat on the floor, punched in the code, and the hatch popped open. Connor kept a close eye on Diesel and committed the five-digit code to memory just in case there was ever a reason to come back here, but he hoped not. "Once you're down, I'll slide down with a little guidance."

"Let's do it. I'll go down first." Connor held a flashlight in one hand and headed down the ladder. Getting Diesel down the ladder was harder than they anticipated. Even with Sullivan guiding him down from the top, it was hard avoiding his leg. The distance was just far enough that pressure on his injured leg was unavoidable. It was a slow process, but they managed to get it done without messing up Diesel's bandage and makeshift cast.

The walk to the manhole leading them back the way they came in a few days ago took longer than Connor expected. He remembered the walk to the bunker took them a while, but it hadn't been that long. They had to stop often for Diesel to rest, and the walking was slow. So slow, Connor swore hours passed with each step.

Climbing the ladder to get out of the manhole was more complicated than getting Diesel down into the tunnel. Despite Connor's objection, Sullivan scouted the area first to find the best route out. Connor didn't like putting Sullivan at risk, but he did have the power of invisibility, making him the logical choice to check the surrounding area before they all climbed out. The bombing left the manhole cover exposed on all sides, and any one of the many soldiers stationed around the area would see them when they climbed out if they weren't careful.

Sullivan returned, identifying a safe path to travel. They still had to rely on Sullivan's power to escape unseen. It wasn't enough to remain invisible—silence was also critical. Silence proved to be more of a challenge than the invisibility. It took both Sullivan and Connor above ground to pull Diesel out. Connor did most of the pulling, while Sullivan focused more on making sure they remained invisible.

Connor thought he'd prepared himself for what he'd see when they surfaced. He heard and felt the bombing for hours, but he was wrong. There was no preparing for what he saw. Everything was flattened, destroyed to nothing more than rubble. The buildings in the Levels were already weak and half-fallen from the last war. Now, they were completely obliterated. Finding a safe path out with cover to hide under was going to be challenging.

Complicating matters more were the number of soldiers patrolling the area. They encountered more soldiers with every turn they took. They needed to move quickly and shift directions fast. With Diesel's handicap and the necessity of invisibility, that proved difficult.

With the degree of destruction, Connor had no way to judge how far they walked or if they were headed in the right direction. All he knew was they had to keep moving. He sensed Diesel's relief when a few standing structures came into view. The streets were still covered in debris and rubble, but it wasn't flattened to the ground. Fewer soldiers patrolled this area as well, making it much easier for them to walk.

Time rushed past and the sun crested in the horizon by the time Connor led them into an abandoned building to rest. Sullivan was fine and managing the pain in his neck well, but Diesel didn't look good. His skin was pale, and his breathing was shallow and raspy.

Connor searched the building and found it was empty. Parts of the top three floors had fallen into the second, and the first floor was mostly covered in debris with a few locations where the ceiling crashed through. A small opening in the rubble led to a storage room. The rubble hid it well behind a treacherous walk with sharp jagged edges around every corner. Connor almost turned back after he started walking the path but spotted the door and decided to continue. It was the perfect place to hide with a low chance of discovery by the wrong person.

As soon as they were safe behind the door, Diesel collapsed. Connor ran to his side and turned him over. "Shit. He's on fire. How does your leg feel? Diesel!"

Diesel didn't respond, his body limp.

Sullivan secured the door and dug out a flashlight. They unwrapped Diesel's bandages. The stitches ripped and white puss seeped out of it. "It's infected. We need to get him to Char," Sullivan said.

"We have at least another half-day journey at this rate. Maybe longer. I really have no idea how far we walked." Connor wiped the sweat off Diesel's forehead. "There's no way he can travel in this condition."

"Go," Sullivan said. "Just go and get my sister. I'll wait here and try to keep him stable."

Connor nodded. "I should be able to make it to her faster

by myself. It depends on how many soldiers I run into. Here, keep these supplies with you. All I need is water."

"Be careful."

"I will. Lock the door behind me and don't open it for anyone but me." Connor slipped out the door and was gone before Sullivan could respond. The sun was up. Without the cover of darkness, his journey back to the hideout would be slower than he liked without Sullivan's power of invisibility. He paused just outside the building and listened. The silence encouraged him, and he took off quickly in the direction of his friends.

CHAPTER SIXTEEN

2031: Day 72, Wednesday

Katrina swallowed her last drop of chicken noodle soup. The hot broth ran down her throat and warmed her from the inside out. She objected when Ajax suggested they stop and prepare a warm meal. She had been fine eating nothing but granola bars and beef jerky, but this soup was just what she needed.

Ajax turned out to be quite resourceful. In the midst of all this destruction, he found an abandoned apartment that still had electricity. He led her to the outer edge of the bombed area where the walking would be easier for her. Another decision she objected to but was grateful she gave into. She argued it was too great a risk walking this edge. The chances of running into people increased the further they moved away from the rubble. It also took them out of the way of her destination. She felt better not having to climb over rocks and large slabs of concrete. She easily forgot about the added distance and to her surprise, they hadn't crossed paths with a single living person.

"Is your special magical ability luck?" Katrina asked with a smile.

"Is that what you think?" He smiled back. "Don't mistake skill for luck."

"Oh, come on, we haven't seen a single person in the two days we've traveled. And you just happen to know where to find electricity. Not to mention, that store was a jackpot. Seems pretty lucky to me."

"Not really, if you think about it." Ajax took her bowl to the kitchen and washed it. "Makes sense that we'd find a safe place with electricity the farther away from the destruction we walked. I'll admit, I'm surprised we haven't seen anyone. My guess is they evacuated this area."

"I guess so." Katrina shrugged. She agreed, but it still seemed too lucky. All of it. Some of it more than others. "But still, let's take how you saved me as an example. How did you carry me so far away from the hideout and get me to the top of that building so fast? It had to take you less than a day to get there and I was passed out. Currently, we've been traveling for two days and still haven't made it back to the hideout."

"So untrusting." Ajax laughed.

It was something that was bothering her since they left yesterday. She had no recollection of how she got there, and it was far away from the hideout. It wasn't a matter of trust. It didn't make sense to her. She stared at him, her lips flat.

"For one, the city had not yet been destroyed when I pulled you out." He dropped his smile and sat next to her. "Most of the bombing occurred after we safely reached the building. Second, I had a motorcycle to take us most of the way. Had to ditch it when a bomb hit the road in front of me and created a giant crater. That was a block or so away from where I took you."

She looked up and met his stare. His eyes pierced through

her, reaching deep within her soul. She tugged at her magic to block her desire to lean towards him, but it disobeyed her. She wasn't even certain it was her desire and not his own magic luring her in.

"I'm not untrusting, just curious." She stood, turning away from him. Her magic may not listen to her, but her body still did.

She found her bag and dug out the pain killers. She didn't really need them, the pain in her ribs was much better. What she needed was a distraction, a reason to pull herself away from Ajax before she lost all control, and this was the first thing that came to mind. Something about the way he looked at her was hard to resist.

"We should head out soon," Ajax said, changing the subject. "It'll be dark soon and we're gonna have to head back into the destruction in another block—maybe two—in order to get back to the hideout. You up for it or would you prefer to stay here for the night?"

"Yep, I'm ready when you're ready. No reason to stop for the night just yet." She swallowed the pills and packed up her bag. Her skin crawled from the stare she knew he still held. She refused to give in to his pull. Instead, she slipped her backpack on and headed for the door. She didn't bother to wait for him to gather his bags. They were two floors up and it would take her longer to walk down than it would take him. Even with her head start, they'd probably reach the ground level about the same time. And if it took him longer, all the better. She needed some distance to regain her composure and control. She hardly knew this man, and all she wanted to do was give herself to him.

KATRINA KEPT HER DISTANCE BEHIND Ajax. An hour or

less passed since they turned back towards the hideout and were forced to maneuver their way through the rubble. He stopped often to give her time to catch up, but she lagged behind again to maintain the space she needed.

He mostly stopped when they reached points where climbing was necessary and she'd need his help to get through the rubble. Those were the moments he put his hands out for support to help her climb over or walk around obstacles. She didn't trust herself that close to him and every time he touched her, even in the slightest, her knees weakened, and all sense of judgment vanished.

The street ahead was a wall of large concrete slabs. A tall building to the right had fallen directly over the path of the street. Ajax walked back and forth, looking for a path. When Katrina reached the wall, she stopped and watched Ajax climb a short section.

"How's it look?" Katrina asked after Ajax climbed back down.

"Not good. I think we're going to have to loop around." He pulled his water bottle out and took a gulp. "It's going to slow us down. I was hoping to make it halfway before stopping for the night."

"Climbing that looks painful, very painful." She looked in each direction. "Which way do you suggest?"

"One is probably just as good as the other." Ajax pointed to the right, the opposite direction of their destination. "Let's head that way and see what we run into."

Katrina nodded and followed his lead. A few buildings in this direction remained standing, and if nothing else, would offer some protection from the elements when they stopped for the night. It would be dark soon, the sun was setting and the shadows were darkening. Another hour at best and it would be too dark to safely travel. Maybe if the moon could shine through there would be enough light to see the hazards, but the sky was too hazy from all the bombing. Even the setting sun was difficult to find behind the dusty blooms filling the air.

With her eyes turned up at the sky, she didn't see Ajax stop and bumped into him. He grabbed her arm to keep her from tumbling to the ground. "Sorry. I was looking up and didn't see you stop."

"Look." He whispered and pointed towards an open area across the street. What was once a solid structure was now replaced with a mound of dead bodies. Her breath caught in her throat and she leaned against the wall behind her for support. This was bound to happen at some point. In the past two days, they hadn't seen a single dead body. While that had surprised her, she hoped everyone escaped without harm. "This explains why we haven't seen the dead."

"But why?" She pulled herself away from the wall and hardened her mind. Her magic encased her body, giving her the strength she needed to look upon the pile of bodies. This was war, and people were dying. She glanced back at the pile and stepped towards it. "Why pile them up like this?"

"Disposal most likely," Ajax said, his voice calm. "My guess is they plan on burning them."

Katrina followed Ajax around the corner and did her best to avoid looking at all the bodies. The dead faces themselves weren't disturbing, she'd seen plenty of dead people in the past. It was the heartless way they were discarded. No remorse, no contacting loved ones, no ceremony of any kind. A single resting place for hundreds burned to ashes with no marker or remembrance of any kind.

If this was war, she didn't want to see any more of it. Knowing this happened and seeing the effects of it firsthand were two very different things. Preparing for this consequence had been part of her training with the Order of Peace, and she thought she could handle it. She was wrong. No amount of training could ever prepare her for the pile of death before her. Nor could that training prepare her for the guilt swelling inside. She glanced back at the pile one last time. Hundreds of lives lost and discarded. How many more piles of dead bodies would she find across the city if she looked? And how many of those dead bodies were her friends?

"Hey." Ajax stopped in front of her. "You okay?"

"Yeah, I'm fine." She lied. "Just tired."

"We'll stop soon for the night." He pointed towards a few buildings remaining ahead. "Those buildings are only a couple blocks away. All we need to do is make it there. We'll find shelter and rest."

She nodded and followed him down a side path that avoided large pieces of fallen concrete. It was still hard walking, but easier than the path they traveled earlier.

The silence of her surroundings bothered her the most, signifying not only the death of people, but the death of the city itself. The city was a noisy place, filled with constant chatter, cars flying by, construction happening around every other corner, or general activities of people working. The only sounds comforting her now were the shuffles of her feet.

Ajax stopped and surveyed the area. He took his time watching each of the buildings ahead and pointed to one that looked like it could be an apartment building. "Let's try that one."

"Ajax." She paused, puzzled by the silence.

"What's wrong?" Ajax turned towards her, a confused look in his eyes.

"The silence. Doesn't it bother you?" She continued walking towards the building he selected. "I know war results in a lot of causalities, but there should still be survivors. I don't like that we haven't seen anyone."

"My guess is they've already cleared this area." He walked beside her for the first time all day. "With the way the dead bodies are piled, I assumed the government relocated any survivors to safe areas."

"I suppose that's possible." She didn't quite believe it. Something felt off, and she couldn't pinpoint what it was. Even her magic was telling her to be careful. Anytime her magic sensed danger, it centered its energy around her chest, which was where all her energy was now. But was it danger or her injury? She struggled with interpreting her magic's intentions and that bothered her almost as much as the silence.

"Come on, let's get inside and make something to eat." Ajax held open the door to the building for Katrina. Inside was a lobby that marked the entrance way for a shopping court. The building may have survived the bombing, but it was a mess from looting. The entire first floor had been ransacked. The furniture was ripped open and turned upside down, and the glass to every business front was broken. There was a stairway to the left marked with mailboxes labeled for each apartment upstairs. "Let's hope upstairs is better than this."

"Are you going to rig up a way to cook me hot soup again?" Katrina asked.

"If that's what you want." He smiled and squeezed her hand before leading the way up the stairs. Her face warmed and her body trembled the moment his hand touched hers. She only hoped he turned away before he saw her face turn red. She tugged her hand away, but he held his grip until they reached the first landing.

"Wait here while I check the doors." Ajax headed down the hall, leaving Katrina standing at the top of the stairs, flustered from his touch. She counted seven doors, three on each side of the hallway and one at the end. Hopefully, one of them would provide the safety they needed for the night.

The looters that destroyed the first floor left a sofa and two chairs on the opposite wall of the landing area intact. Seeing the sofa made her legs scream in pain and exhaustion. She pushed herself too hard today and should have listened to Ajax about healing herself before starting this journey.

She walked over to the sofa and let her body fall into the cushions. She leaned her head onto the back edge and heard a loud cracking noise like a tree branch snapping. Before she lifted her head up, the floor beneath the sofa gave way, and the wall behind her crumbled to the ground. An involuntary, loud yelp escaped her mouth when the sofa sank down in one quick swoop and then slammed to a stop.

More pain rushed through her body and knocked the air out of her. Her eyes locked shut and her chest would not take in air. Crippled from pain and disoriented by the swiftness of the fall, she remained frozen on the sofa. This fall was going to be her end—she was going to die. After all she had survived the past few months, this seemed like a stupid way to meet her end. The pain faded and a tingling sensation washed over her, leaving her in a state of paralysis. She dug deep within searching for her magic and couldn't find it. The jar to her body had been too much and she drifted into the darkness.

A tug and a name, followed by a spark of light, caused her body to twitch.

"Katrina," Ajax yelled.

Louder still, his voice called to her. Her lungs opened and she gasped for air. Her body acted independent of her and the deep breath sent a forceful pain through her. She doubled over in pain and the sofa beneath her jerked then slid down further.

"Don't move," Ajax yelled. "You're caught in mid-air."

Katrina opened her eyes and everything was a blur. She focused her eyes on the movement and bits of flashing light surrounded by darkness. She blinked several times until her eyes focused on the light, and the darkness faded. Ajax reached down, both arms stretched out before her. *How is he so close?* She should be laying on the ground level of the first floor, out of his reach. She shifted her head from side to side, and the answer came quickly. When the wall behind her broke away, the column below slanted outward and stopped her from falling all the way down to the floor.

"Take my hand." Ajax stretched further, trying to grab her hand. Her hand lifted to meet his and the couch slipped further down. The column suspending her in air cracked, giving way to the weight piled on top of it. Ajax wrapped his hand tight around hers and pulled. Her body lifted off the sofa just as the column gave out and tumbled to the ground. She let out a loud scream. Her body hung down, the only thing holding her up was Ajax's grip.

"Give me your other hand," Ajax yelled down to her. She tried but failed. The pain in her chest was more than she could take and she didn't have the strength to lift her other arm. Her hand slipped under his grip and her eyes swelled with tears.

Ajax wrapped his free hand around her wrist and tightened his grip. An unfamiliar weight pushed against her back, stopping her from slipping further down. Her magic rushed to protect her, as it always did, and provided an invisible barrier.

A calmness settled on her heart and a faint whisper blew in her ear. *Call the wind.* The words rang through her mind and she understood. Her physical form may not have the strength to lift herself up, but her elemental power did. All she had to do was call upon it to do her will.

Her body stiffened and her free hand swung up then wrapped around Ajax's arm. She opened her eyes and met his stare. The desperation and fear she read in his eyes shifted to determination. The slight breeze her magic brought to her transitioned into a strong gust, giving her the additional boost Ajax needed to pull her up to safety.

He pulled her away from the edge and held her tight. "I've got you," he whispered into her ear. She turned her head towards his and their eyes met again. Her heart fluttered and an unrecognizable tingling sensation replaced all the pain in her chest. This time she didn't fight it, she gave into the strange feelings she didn't quite understand.

She leaned into Ajax, and he dropped his head then rested his forehead on hers. His breath brushed across her cheek and without thinking, she lifted her lips to his. Soft and gentle, his lips returned her kiss and he tightened his arms around her. Her whole body screamed to be closer to him.

His lips felt like nothing she had ever felt before. Exciting, soft, yet strong.

Time stopped. She pressed her body closer to his, eliminating the space between them. Nothing else existed in this moment except him and his kisses. The fear crippling her mere moments ago was a distant memory, and all her pain was gone. There was only him.

He pulled his lips away, lifting his head to gaze into her eyes. She lifted her head with his, refusing to let go of his lips.

"Not yet," she whispered. Her lips met his again, pulling him back in—but only for a moment.

"As much as I've been waiting for this moment," Ajax said. He brushed his lips along her cheek and chin, then down the thin line of her neck. "I need to make sure you're not hurt."

"Oh, I'm fine." She chuckled.

"You say that now, but later you may regret this." Ajax released her. He lent her a hand, picked her up, and held her close. "Let's go check your injuries and then feed you."

Katrina's body fell into his and she let his weight carry her to an empty apartment on the opposite side of the building. For the first time in years, she relied fully on another person. She let him carry her to a bed, take her shoes off, and check her over for any new injuries. Thankfully, there were none. He gave her medicine and tucked her in. She curled up and waited, still wrapped in the warmth of his kiss, for him to bring her hot soup.

That night she slept wrapped in his arms. Curled up close to his body was a comfort she never knew she should long for. Now that she had him here, wrapped in the comfort and security of his embrace, she never wanted to let him go.

CHAPTER SEVENTEEN

2031: Day 72, Wednesday

The day had been long and tiring. Connor underestimated how difficult the walk back to the hideout would be, and exhaustion took over. His eyes were heavy and his legs were sore. The smart thing to do would be to stop and rest, but he continued pushing himself forward.

He already slipped several times climbing over rocks and debris, slicing his hand open. Blood, once again, seeped out the side of his bandage and he had to stop to redress it. He ducked into the remnants of a building and hid behind a half wall. The moment he sat down, sleep fought to take over.

Unfortunately, he didn't bring much with him and left all the medical supplies with Sullivan and Diesel. He should have known to prepare. All he had was a half tube of ointment. The ointment helped, but he had to rip fabric off his shirt to wrap the cut and minimize the bleeding. It wasn't the best bandage he'd ever seen, but it worked.

He had enough food, but he'd need to find more water.

He may have had enough to make the trip had he not cut his hand, but he had to use his water to clean his cut. If the cut got infected, that would probably kill him before low water supply. He'd find more water, but an infection he couldn't do a lot about. He already refilled his water bottles once today. Broken water pipes leaked all over the city. So long as they didn't run dry anytime soon, he'd be fine.

He ate a few bites and took a sip of water before packing up and standing. If he sat much longer, there'd be no getting back up tonight, and delaying another night was not an option. The sooner he made it back to the hideout, the sooner he could find his friends and save Ebony.

Ebony. He tried not to let his brain drift to her. Every time thoughts of her surfaced, he pushed them aside. But now, in his exhausted state, she was there, and he couldn't do anything about it. Worse, he couldn't push out the horrors he imagined Dr. Hunter doing to her.

He slipped his bag over his shoulder and started on his journey once more. Now that Ebony had entered the forefront of his mind, he was distracted. He tripped over a rock, stubbing his big toe. Frustrated with himself, he forced himself to focus on the dangerous ground before him, but his focus came a moment too late. He stepped out on the main road and two soldiers stood before him.

"Well, well, well," the shorter of the two said. "Who do we have here."

"I'll check the pictures." The second guard, much taller and more muscular than the first, pulled a pad out of his pocket and scrolled through images. "He's so filthy I can't tell."

The shorter guard lifted his gun and pressed it against Connor's chest. "We'll take him anyway. If he is important, we'll collect the reward and be done with this shit job."

"I don't know who you're looking for, but I can assure you

I am not him." Connor didn't wait for a response. He used the last bit of his energy to draw his magic out and enter both of their minds. The taller one immediately stepped aside to let him pass, but the shorter one stood his ground. A closed-lip smile crept across his face.

"So we do have someone important." With his free hand, the short soldier slapped the taller one on the side of his head. "Snap out of it, Bill."

"Hey." Bill rubbed the side of his head. "What'd you do that for?"

"This one used his magic on you. Mind control, same as the one we're looking for." The soldier pressed his gun deeper into Connor's chest. "Get on your knees."

"You're mistaken," Connor said. He complied with the orders to get the soldier to pull his gun back. The short one was a strong Magical Bond and most likely trained on what to look for when questioning suspects, but the taller one, Bill, was Common Blood. As tired as Connor was, it would not be easy getting out of this. Unlike him, these two looked well rested.

"Mistakes get sorted out at base. If we're wrong, they'll set you free, but we're taking you in." He unhooked a pair of handcuffs from his belt and handed them to Bill. "Cuff him."

Connor kept his eyes on the gun still pointed at his chest. He couldn't get a read on this guy to know if he would shoot him for fighting back. For all he knew, orders were to kill if suspects resisted arrest. One thing was for certain, he couldn't let those handcuffs reach his arms. He shifted his attention to Bill and took control of his mind and body. It was an easy takeover despite his tired state. Bill may be a big guy, but he wasn't very bright, and the slow-witted ones were always the easiest to control.

Connor forced him to toss the handcuffs aside where they

fell into a pile of rocks. This was enough to distract the short one and for Bill to rush into him, knocking him to the ground. Connor took this chance to run. He pushed himself to run faster than he'd ever run before, but he feared he couldn't run fast enough. He managed to put distance between him and the soldiers and for now, that was enough. He glanced over his shoulder and Bill still had the small guy on the ground. So long as Connor's control hung on long enough for him to hide, he might just get out of this.

But where to hide?

If they suspected he was the one that infiltrated Research Island, they'd tear this area apart in search of him. He ran as hard as he could down a side alley. It was blocked by large boulders, but he didn't let that stop him.

There was yelling not far behind him. The soldiers were up and chasing after him, most likely with backup on the way. Connor glanced over his shoulder one last time before he hopped over the top of the boulder. It was all clear. He made it over the top before they reached him.

He jumped over too fast and instead of a controlled decline down the other side, he slid to the bottom. His head knocked into the side of the concrete several times and his body scraped along several sharp edges before he came to a stop. For a moment, he was breathless and stunned. The slide down the boulder knocked the wind out of him and he couldn't move. He hit his head so hard when he hit the bottom, he saw stars.

The voices from the soldiers were louder and multiplied. The two that found him called in support. It would be an all-out manhunt to find him. He should have stayed put for the night. He knew better than to push himself this hard. He had been in no condition to continue on and now look at him. His body was scraped up and his head was bleeding.

"Shit." He pressed his hand on his head. The rock gouged the side of his head above his left ear. Blood ran around his ear and down the side of his neck, but there was no time to tend to that now. He had to get up and run before they found him.

Slowly, he stood and walked across the street, perpendicular to the path to the hideout. If he headed a few streets over, he might stand a chance at losing the soldiers. He cut through another alley and was forced to stop. His vision blurred and he lost his balance. His back fell towards the wall behind him, and he pressed his eyes closed. If he didn't gain control of his spinning head, he would pass out. His body swayed, and the world around him spun like a wind tunnel. He had no idea how long he stood still—however long it took for him to stop spinning. When he opened his eyes again, he strained to focus on the ground beneath his feet.

Reality hit him hard. He had to find a place to hide—now. He hit his head too hard and if he tried to continue any farther, he would be caught. The sun was setting, and the darkness of night was all he had working in his favor.

Using the wall behind him for support, he walked to the end of the alley. The building supporting him was intact and he slipped through the door on the front. It was a clothing store. He pulled a couple shirts off a rack and stumbled towards the back of the store. In the back were three fitting rooms. Connor slipped into one and locked the door behind him. It wasn't the best hiding place, but it would have to do.

He slid his backpack off and dug around until he found his flashlight and water bottle. Wetting the corner of one of the shirts he grabbed, he wiped his head clean. The other shirt, he ripped into strips and wrapped it around his head as a bandage.

He turned off the flashlight and listened. Silence surrounded him. With any luck, he was safe for the night. He tossed his backpack onto the floor and laid down, resting his head on it. His eyes closed the moment his head hit his pack. It didn't matter if he wanted them closed or not. Exhaustion took over, and he slept.

CHAPTER EIGHTEEN

2031: Day 73, Early Thursday

The morning sun blinded Connor. His tired eyes refused to open when he stepped out onto the street in front of the clothing shop. It was quiet and still, not even the slightest gust from the wind to provide him company. In his panicked state last night, he hadn't noticed most of the buildings on this street were still intact. In one direction, the city showed no signs of war. In the direction of the underground hideout, however, the city was obliterated. Hardly a structure remained standing. The rest of his path back would be treacherous, and more exhausting than yesterday's walk.

He slept the entire night undisturbed. Either his hiding spot was better than he thought, or the soldiers gave up and never started a full search. He hoped the latter was the case. With any luck, the soldiers were too embarrassed for having lost him and never called in for assistance. If they had called it in, the hunt for him would continue today, making his travels more dangerous than they already were. He refused to let himself think about that. He had to keep going and assume the best. It was the only way he'd make it the rest of the way.

Convincing himself he was safe, he slipped back inside the shop to clean his injuries and put on fresh bandages. With his new head injury, he'd forgotten about the cut on his hand. This morning his hand hurt worse than his head. He was light-headed, but that could've been from the hard night sleep. At least that's what he told himself.

This morning, he grabbed a couple more shirts, this time picking softer t-shirts, and found a bathroom in the back of the store. Last night, he took the first shirt he saw and it was rough and scratchy against his skin. To his surprise, the water still ran in this part of the city. A welcome treat and luxury he dearly missed. It was odd how something as simple as water had become a luxury these past few days. It reminded him of his younger days after he ran away from the orphanage. For a year he had lived without running water, bathing mostly in lakes or streams and stealing his drinking water from nearby gas stations and grocery stores. That year had been rough, and he had no desire to return to that way of life.

Connor stepped back outside, his eyes ready for the bright sun. With fresh bandages and a full supply of water, he was ready to restart his journey. Losing the weight of Diesel and his injury did nothing to speed up his journey. He expected to move quickly through the side streets and alleys, but the extent of yesterday's bombing was more widespread than he imagined. And he thought he had imagined the worst.

The newly inflicted destruction pocketed the landscape of the city. Every block, he found himself at the edge of desolation. Every building, every street sign, every trace of human life was reduced to a flattened layer of dust and rubble. He never wanted another war and had hoped to end the oppression on the Common Blood with minimal damage. So much for that hope.

Minimal damage. Was that even a thing? He was foolish

to even think such words. His city had already sustained more damage than it could handle. Every building for about twenty blocks or more was destroyed. It wasn't nearly as large an area as the Levels, but still significant and much closer to Manhattan. When the government bombed the Levels in 2018, they only took out Common Blood. Not this time. This bombing showed the government's desperation in taking out the rebels. Just based on the area bomb, more Magical Bond died in this war than Common Blood.

He didn't know how it was possible, but the destruction was worse the closer he got to the hideout. Any hope he had of finding Katrina and Charlotte alive were crushed. He was forced to continue underground via the subway tunnels. It wasn't safe to walk across the leveled landscape. The ground swayed beneath his feet and there was no cover to protect him from discovery. When he turned the corner at the edge of the last standing structure, he saw small groups of soldiers patrolling the perimeter of flattened streets. He assumed they were on the lookout for survivors. For all he knew these soldiers were looking for him.

The subway tunnels proved to be just as difficult but at least there were no soldiers down here. The train route was buried in the middle of a bombed three-block radius. Everything was gone, sunken into the deep hole that took the subway tunnels with it. He had no choice but to go deeper into tunnels he'd never traveled before. By the looks of them, he guessed no one had accessed them for years. Out of fear of getting lost, he poked his head through a manhole access point to check his surroundings and look for landmarks he recognized. Recognizing anything proved to be futile. The only thing he could confirm was he was still following the subway tracks that led to the hideout.

He pulled himself through the last manhole he checked. The hideout was near, his magic sensed the closeness. If his judge of distance was correct, the area above the hideout took a direct hit. That didn't look good for his friends and the thought of losing another friend caused him to buckle over. He still struggled with losing Ness and Lina, losing Katrina too would send him over the edge. Taking a deep breath, he forced himself to stand tall. He would not let grief stop him now.

He reached a point where even the subway tracks were gone. The rubble from above tumbled into the deep, unused tunnels and took the tracks with it. He had no choice but to climb up to the surface and risk being seen. As it turned out, there was no risk. Only a fool would attempt to walk this area, and the distance to the patrolled streets was too great for anyone to see him climbing around these rocks.

The further he walked, the more it tormented his mind. The more tormented his mind, the clumsier he became. He rushed where he should heed caution and slipped onto sharp jagged rocks. He managed to avoid more cuts, but he was sure to be covered in bruises. He could no longer control his thoughts. With the state of this area, it was impossible to stop his negative thoughts from consuming him. He had to find a way to center himself again if he hoped to continue. He climbed down the rubble mess somewhere between the surface and the subway tracks and crawled into a small nook between two slabs of concrete. He leaned his head back, eyes closed, and called upon the calming powers of his magic.

Magic. He hadn't thought about Vivian's ban on magic since they left Diesel's bunker under the hospital. He never thought she would take it to that level. It shouldn't have surprised him, but it did. Unsanctioned use of magic only created a deeper wedge between the Magical Bond and Common Blood. It made him and his friends the threat and it made her look like she cared about the Common Blood. A bold move on her part considering all she wanted was to be magical, to control all magic for herself. She despised people like him, born with powerful magic. She would do anything to have his power—even blow up a large part of the city to try to gain it.

He should have anticipated this. Vivian Way was all about appearances, and she wanted to appear as the citizen's savior even if her purpose was to destroy them all. She chose every word wisely, making people feel comforted and safe. It didn't matter that it was a lie, it didn't even matter if they knew it would never become reality. All that mattered was they believed she understood their needs, their concerns, and their oppression. Everything she did and said was a game and the citizens were a tool to serve her needs. Her actions undermined the people's very existence and that angered Connor most of all. They were oppressed, but not for the reasons Vivian made them believe. Their oppression was by design, the driving force behind every decision Vivian made. All because they had no magic.

All this focus on Vivian was not helping Connor calm his mind. It only exhausted him more and made him angry. He slipped out from his resting spot and continued towards the subway entrance closest to the hideout. He was almost there. One more large bolder and he should see it. He pulled himself up to the top and an involuntary smile took over his face. Relief and hope filled his heart.

The subway landing near the hideouts tunnel was intact.

The tunnel was quiet and dark. As the tunnel curved back in the direction of the hideout, beams of light found the cracks created by the bombing from above. The ceiling wasn't stable and with every step he took, he feared the ceiling would crumble down on top of him.

The floor beneath him was covered in dust but quickly transitioned to nothing but large rock and debris. The hope he felt moments ago withered away. His path became a maze of crawling over and under large boulders then squeezing through tight spots. His heart sank when he turned the last corner and saw the front entrance to the hideout completely blown away.

CHAPTER NINETEEN

2031: Day 73, Evening Thursday

Connor fell to his knees, his eyes full of tears. The hideout was nothing more than a crumbled pile of rock, concrete, and twisted rebar. A few passageways were visible, but the walls fell in on themselves and the ceiling was scattered in pieces. He didn't need to walk through the debris to see the dead bodies trapped under the rock and concrete. Every direction he pointed his flashlight, a vacant face stared back at him. The dust that settled on the room painted every face a pale gray, making them indistinguishable from one another.

No one could survive a blast that did this much damage.

The unrecognizable death surrounding him sucked all the remaining energy Connor had left. He pushed himself up to his feet anyway. Katrina and Charlotte had to be here and he would find their bodies. He didn't care about getting caught or that he was too exhausted and hurt himself. His safety no longer mattered. His life no longer mattered. All hope he had for the future was gone along with the lives of the ones he loved the most.

Most of the bodies were mutilated and crushed by the falling rock, but some of them were covered with multiple gunshot wounds. Despite the gruesome condition of the bodies, seeing gunshot wounds gave him hope. SUM made a direct hit and sent in soldiers to take out the resistance. There was the possibility that SUM captured Katrina and Charlotte and they were not among the lifeless bodies trapped in the debris. Maybe it was too much to hope for, but that tiny spark of hope was enough to energize his power and clear his mind of the negative thoughts. Regardless of the outcome, he could not let SUM crush his soul into oblivion. Sullivan was still out there and Ebony still needed rescuing.

The burst of energy Connor's magic sent through his body faded quickly. His legs and hands turned numb. He clenched his fingers into fists and stomped his feet to bring them back to life. He needed to get back to Sullivan and formulate a plan. Sullivan would not respond well to the news about his sister. The unknown of whether or not she was even alive would torment him. Connor had already been gone much longer than anticipated, and Sullivan probably already assumed the worse.

A sound behind him caught his ear. Connor pulled his gun from his hip and turned to face it. He heard it again—the sound of small rocks falling. He ducked behind a large slab of concrete and aimed his gun in the direction of the sound, but the darkness made it impossible to see anything.

"ARE YOU SURE YOU WANT TO CLIMB down there?" Ajax shined the flashlight into the pit that once was the hideout.

"Yes," Katrina said, her voice flat. She had to go down there. If there was any chance of finding Connor, this was it.

It didn't look promising, but she had to try. "How did you get me out of there?"

There were no paths, no stairs, just piles of rock and concrete. With the sun beginning to set, it looked even more horrifying, like climbing down the side of a vertical cliff freehand.

"Well," Ajax chuckled. "It wasn't easy and involved a lot of tugging."

She rolled her eyes at him and tightened the straps to her backpack. This was going to hurt. Maybe more so than her near-death experience with the collapsing wall yesterday. If she lost her grip, even for a second, it could mean death. *You can do this. Just a little further.* If Connor was down there, she had to make it the rest of the way. She took a deep breath and slid down the side of the first edge. Her feet found solid rock quicker than expected. Shifting to the side, she made room for Ajax to follow.

"I'm surprised there are no soldiers or guards here." Katrina sat on the ground and slid herself down to the next ledge. "This was our last known location. It seems logical to keep a close eye on it, just in case we returned."

"Maybe they assumed you were dead," Ajax said as his feet landed behind hers.

"Maybe." She shrugged, not sure she believed that. SUM never assumed anything. Knowing SUM, they planned this entire war and she was meant to be left behind to search for Connor. Ajax wouldn't understand. He wasn't on the island and he didn't see firsthand just how sinister SUM was. If they could plan out their entire lives, they could certainly plan out this war and hunt them down.

Katrina decided against telling Ajax what happened on the island. He'd asked her several times in different ways to get her to talk, but she refused. At first, it was because she didn't trust him, now it was because she didn't want to relive those events.

"Hey, you with me?" Ajax brushed his hand across her cheek, drawing her eyes to his. He leaned in and pressed his lips into hers. His touch was all it took. She melted into him and for a second forgot where she was. He pulled back and stared into her eyes. "We don't have to do this. I don't want to see you in more pain."

"I know you don't." Her hands trembled, more from the closeness of his body than the uncertainty of what she'd find at the bottom of this pit. "But yes, I do have to do this."

She pulled her body away from his and shined the flashlight down, looking for the next ledge to climb down to. Any natural light they did have from the sun was gone and darkness consumed them. The deeper they crawled, the cooler it became. Katrina looked back at Ajax. His arms were covered in goose bumps. He had gotten hot during their walk here and he never put his jacket back on. She tugged at the warmth of her elemental power and spread it around her. She dug deeper and created a wider band of warmth that reached Ajax as well. Hopefully, it'd be enough to keep the chill off him until they reached the bottom and it was safe to get his jacket out of his bag. It was the least she could do considering how many times he saved her life.

A FLASH OF LIGHT AND A GLIMPSE of movement made Connor's body stiffen. He leaned his body forward, pressing it into the concrete and held his breath. His finger tensed on the trigger, ready to shoot.

"I don't think anyone is here," an unfamiliar male voice said. The flashlight one of them carried illuminated the figure in front of them. He strained to focus his eyes, but the brightness of the light made it impossible to see.

"Then we'll wait, see if he shows up," Katrina said.

"Kat," Connor whispered and moved out from behind the slab. The figure rushed towards him, and her face came into view. "You're alive!"

He ran to her and hugged her tightly.

"Just barely." Her voiced strained and she winced under his embrace.

"Are you hurt?" Connor stepped back to look at her, but it was too dark to see anything.

"I could be worse, I suppose. I have a few broken ribs and ache all over." Her faced beamed and despite Connor's worry, he smiled back at her. "A lot of rock landed on me when they blasted through the doors."

"Charlotte?" Connor asked. The smile on Katrina's face faded. He knew the answer without asking. If she had been with them, she would have healed Katrina's wounds.

"We were ambushed in the middle of the night." Katrina slid her backpack off and pulled out her water bottle. "They took Char. I saw that much before I passed out. Didn't see much else though."

"So she's alive." His shoulders relaxed and most of the tension in his neck eased. This wasn't good news, but at least he didn't have to go back and tell Sullivan his sister was dead. "Why didn't they take you?"

"Don't know. Either they didn't care about me or they assumed I was dead." She shrugged. "It's also possible they didn't know I was there. I was in the back and got buried in the first blast."

"Well, thank goodness you're okay." Connor leaned next to her and wrapped his arm around her shoulder. "When I got here, well...there are no words for how I felt."

Connor didn't want to think about death anymore. He didn't want to speculate emotions or deal with the ones he struggled with already. He was happy Katrina was alive and he would focus on that.

"Is Sullivan here?" Katrina asked.

"No, I left him with Diesel a good ways from here. Diesel's leg is injured. He couldn't walk on his own and slowed me down." Katrina's expression shifted to anger at the mention of Diesel. Putting the two of them in a confined room together wasn't going to be easy and Connor knew it. He'd never forget how Diesel's past actions impacted Katrina.

"He helped Sullivan, Kat," Connor said. "No matter how you feel about him, he's still a great surgeon."

"But Sully's okay?" she asked. "That's all that really matters."

"Yeah." Connor dropped his head into his hand and rubbed his forehead. "At least until he finds out Char has been taken."

A rock rolled across the ground from the direction Katrina had come. Connor tensed, pulled his gun back out, and stared at the darkness. He had forgotten about the male voice he heard before he saw Katrina. "Who's with you?"

"Ajax." She coughed. The gray dust that covered every inch of the hideout stirred with each movement and floated into the air.

"Who's Ajax?" Connor asked, gripping his gun close to his side. He took two steps forward, shielding Katrina from the person standing at the edge of the shadows.

"Connor." Katrina's voice was hoarse. She pulled his arm, but he shrugged her off and moved towards Ajax. "He's okay. He saved me."

Her words did nothing to stop Connor. He lunged

forward and pushed Ajax up against the slab of concrete opposite them and pressed his arm into his neck. Connor held his fist in the air, ready to punch him, but Katrina wielded her magic and threw a burst of fire at Connor. Light orange flames surrounded Connor's fist. He jumped back, waving his hand in the air until the flames went out.

"What the hell, Kat." He glanced back at her. Katrina had never used her magic on him outside of training.

"You're fine." She walked over to Ajax and wrapped her arms around his chest. Ajax leaned down and kissed to the top of her head. "Those were show flames, no danger of burning you."

Connor rubbed his hand and inspected it as best he could with the flashlight. He didn't have any blistering, and as far as he could tell his only injury was to his ego.

He couldn't believe what he was seeing. It had been less than a week since he left her at the hideout and here she was hugging this strange man. He turned his back to her, coughing now himself. His throat was dry and sore from inhaling too much dust. He swallowed the last of his water, but it wasn't enough to relieve his throat.

"Here, take this." Katrina handed him a full bottle.

"You keep that. Who knows when we'll find more."

"We have plenty." Katrina smiled and dropped the bottle in his hand, refusing to let him deny her. "Are you ready to listen to me?"

Connor didn't speak, only slightly nodded his head to say yes.

Katrina stepped forward and took Connor's hand in her own. He remained tense and didn't return the squeeze she gave. He kept his eyes on Ajax, watching his face carefully. Katrina cupped her hands on his cheeks, forcing Connor to look at her. "Ajax saved me. After SUM took Char, they all left. I was stuck under a slab and couldn't get free. He also survived and got me out of here, took me somewhere safe so I could heal. He found lots of food and water. Enough to get us through a week, maybe more."

Connor frowned and pulled away. He didn't like that she'd showed up with a stranger or that she hugged him the way she did. Bringing an outsider in was a risk they couldn't afford. Connor pulled Katrina aside, out of earshot of Ajax. "Look, I appreciate that he helped you, but how do you know you can trust him?"

"Not everyone is bad." Katrina shrugged his hand off her arm. "I know you worry, but he's okay. If he wasn't, my magic would tell me."

"And what was that hug about?" Connor took a deep breath. "You have a crush, don't you?"

"I'm not a child," she said, her voice louder than before. "I can make decisions for myself."

"Well, I...don't...like it," he said between coughs.

"You'll get over it." She took the water bottle she handed him and unscrewed the lid before handing it back. "Drink it. All of it."

"No, save some for yourself." He shoved it back.

"I told you, we've got plenty and know where we can get more." She pushed the bottle into his chest. "Stop being such a stubborn ass."

He jerked the bottle from her, splashing some of it down his shirt. Without further objection, he drank the entire bottle in one long swig. It was the most he'd drank in two days. Dehydration was starting to drag him down and this water was exactly what he needed.

"Thanks," he said, screwing the lid back on the bottle.

"It's been a long day and we all look like we could use some rest. Get comfortable, we'll leave after everyone's gotten some sleep."

Katrina smiled and handed Connor another bottle of water. "Here, drink more. You look like you could use it."

Connor ignored her and slid down the wall opposite her. He kicked his legs out in front of him and closed his eyes.

"When's the last time you ate?" Katrina asked.

"I don't know. I've lost track of the days." He tried to put a time frame on the events of the past several days and he couldn't. His head pounded from the injury he sustained yesterday. At least he thought it was yesterday. "I can't even remember when we left Diesel's bunker and headed this way. It might've been this morning, it might've been two days ago. Time is a haze."

"Here, start with this." Ajax spoke for the first time since they arrived. He held a granola bar in his hand. Connor glared at him and tried to use his magic to read Ajax's mind. Nothing happened. The pain in his head only ached worse when he called upon his magic. He was too weak and his head injury interfered. "We raided a pharmacy and cleaned them out of pain killers and antibiotics. Maybe these might work."

Connor held his eyes on Ajax's face when he handed him a box of pain killers. He didn't speak and didn't move to take them. Katrina had always been too trusting of people and he saw no reason to trust this man, not until he proved himself worthy of trust. They had enough problems to solve and Connor hoped Ajax wouldn't cause them more.

"Be nice." Katrina punched him in the arm. Ajax placed the box by Connor's leg and stepped back.

"What?" He turned his glare towards her.

"You know what. Stop it." She slouched down next to

him. "I know you're just being protective, but let it go. For me."

"Fine." Connor opened the box and swallowed two pain killers. He was so thirsty, he drank all of the other bottle she had given him. "Thanks."

"Sully's going to flip when he finds out about Char."

"Probably." Connor's eyes met hers. Diesel needed Charlotte's healing power and may very well die without it. But Katrina probably didn't care about that. She wanted Diesel dead. Even with the antibiotics they had, it may be too late to do any good.

"I see that look in your eye," Katrina said. "This wasn't your fault."

"How can it not be my fault? Look around, Kat. Our friends are dead, the Order has been destroyed, more of the city has been flattened, and Char is gone. All because we went to research island on my order. Please explain to me how this isn't my fault."

"You had no way of knowing this would happen."

"It was my plan. If I listened to the council, maybe I could've spared Ness and Lina. Maybe none of this would've happened, and the Order would still be alive."

"So what?" She shrugged, her voice calm. "It doesn't matter whose plan it was, we did this together and the outcome would've been the same no matter what. This was going to happen eventually no matter what we did or didn't do. SUM has always had the upper hand."

"You don't understand."

"I do understand," Katrina said. "No one could've controlled this situation, not even you. Yeah, maybe our actions made SUM move faster, but it didn't change a damn thing. This would've happened eventually."

Connor started to argue back but stopped himself. It

didn't matter to him if SUM would have eventually done this or not. His actions triggered it now, and he couldn't do anything to bring back the ones lost. But he could try and get Ebony and Charlotte back. That was something he could do and doing something was better than doing nothing.

CHAPTER TWENTY

2031: Day 74, Late Friday

Connor squeezed through the thin passage that led to the storage closet where he left Sullivan and Diesel. Katrina and Ajax followed close behind. Their travel back didn't take nearly as long as it had taken Connor to make his way to the hideout.

To save time, they cut through the rubble in the most direct path back. The walk was faster even with the obstacles of remnant walls and large piles of rock. By taking this path, they avoided the soldiers as well. It was a hard and hostile journey, but they made it back without getting caught.

Katrina kept up and did her best to hide her pain, but Connor saw every bit of it on her face. She did fine when the ground was flat, but every time they had to climb it was a challenge for her. Despite her pain, she never once complained. A few more turns then they would reunite with Sullivan and Diesel and she could rest.

Connor turned the last corner and looked over his

shoulder to watch for Katrina. It was a tricky turn with several jagged rocks protruding from hazardous walls made of large boulders. The lack of light made it even more challenging to maneuver the path without additional injuries. He didn't realize he was holding his breath until her hand wrapped around the rock. He stepped back to offer her support, but Ajax leaned in close against her body from the other side, making his offer unnecessary.

A frown involuntarily took over his face. It shouldn't bother him, but Connor couldn't stand to see Ajax with her. He couldn't put his finger on it, and his magic wasn't helpful. No matter how hard he tried, his magic couldn't enter Ajax's mind. He was blocked every time. What he did know was his magic warned him to be careful and kept his defenses on high alert.

He tried to push his mistrust of Ajax aside for Katrina, but he couldn't change how his magic responded. She insisted her magic drew her closer to Ajax, but his magic was ready to fight him. Ajax was a risk, a danger, and Connor trusted his own magic more than hers.

For her sake, Connor attempted to be nice, but he wouldn't let his guard down. Until Ajax earned his place among their ranks and proved to his magic he was trustworthy, he'd keep a close watch on him.

"Here, give me your hand." Connor reached out to offer her support from his side. "Just a few more steps and you're there."

Katrina reached her hand out and collapsed into him. She had pushed herself too hard today and her body gave out. Connor lodged his foot into the side of a rock to maintain his balance and take on all of her weight while she worked her way through the rest of the way.

"I got you," he said. "Let's get you inside where you can

rest." Connor turned and stopped in front of a closed door and rapped lightly. The same light rap echoed from inside the door.

"Connor Vance."

The door clicked and slowly opened revealing a dark room, the only light came from a dim candle burning in the corner.

"Man, what took you so long?" Sullivan grabbed hold of Connor and gave him a tight hug, catching Connor off guard. The two of them had never been chummy and a hug was the last thing he'd expected.

"It's a lot worse out there than I expected." Connor slipped his backpack off and tossed it to the ground. He was more exhausted than he realized. All he wanted to do was fall to the ground and sleep, but his duty wasn't done. "Soldiers were everywhere and...well...how do I say this? The hideout was destroyed."

"What do you mean destroyed?" Sullivan looked to the door and shined a flashlight at Katrina and Ajax. He pushed them aside and ran out of the doorway. "Where's Char?"

"Sully." Katrina reached for his arm but he pulled away. "She's alive, but she was taken by SUM."

"What do you mean taken?" He pushed back through the door, knocking Ajax to the ground. "Connor, you said you'd get her."

Connor blocked Sullivan's path, but he pushed him, knocking him to the ground, too. Sullivan paced back and forth in the small space available and ended up going in circles. Connor's legs didn't want to obey him after days of constant abuse, so he remained on the ground. "Try to stay calm. We'll get her back, Sully. We will."

"Try to stay calm," he yelled. He grabbed his backpack

and ran towards the passageway. The tight spaces and hazardous conditions stopped Sullivan from getting past the first corner, giving Connor time to push himself up and catch him. Sullivan collapsed on the ground, tears running down his cheeks. "She's all I have, all I've ever had," he said.

"You have us now, too." Connor spoke in a calm, reassuring voice. "We're in this together and we'll help you get her back."

"I let them put that stupid tracker in my neck and led them to her. I should've resisted." His voice trailed off, and his body relaxed.

"Come on. Let's get behind this door and rest. We'll make a plan, together, after a hot meal and a good night's sleep." Connor helped him up and walked him into the room. Katrina shut the door and locked it. Ajax turned on a battery-powered lantern he'd taken from the convenience store they looted, adding considerable light to the room.

Katrina sat with Sullivan, saying nothing. There was no use trying to talk to him right now. He needed to come to terms with this in his own time and nothing they said was going to make a bit of difference. While Katrina did her best to comfort Sullivan, Connor checked on Diesel.

Diesel was asleep on the floor and hadn't stirred with all the commotion. His fever persisted and his body was clammy. Rest and antibiotics were the best Connor could offer him. Hopefully, that'd be enough. "How long has he been like this?"

"Since you left. He fell asleep and only woke to drink water and take more meds." Sullivan leaned his head back against the wall and stretched his legs out in front of him. "Not sure how long he'll stay like this though, we're out of meds and almost out of water."

"No worries," Ajax said. "We've got plenty of both. Plenty of food, too."

"Who are you?" Sullivan blurted out.

"Ajax." He held his hand out, offering a shake. Sullivan stared at him and made no move to accept his hand.

"Ajax saved my life. He got me out after SUM attacked," Katrina said. "We were the only ones that got away. They took Char and killed everyone else."

"Lucky you." Sullivan glared at Ajax before turning his eyes to Connor. Connor nodded, understanding Sullivan's thoughts. He too wasn't happy about this stranger joining them.

WITH GROGGY EYES AND A PAINFUL yawn, Katrina pushed herself up to a seated position. Her breath caught from the sharp jab in her side. Sleeping on the hard, concrete floor didn't do her ribs any favors, and she didn't feel particularly rested. She should have taken something stronger for her pain before she crashed, but exhaustion won out, and she collapsed soon after they arrived. She welcomed the exhaustion. It forced sleep where otherwise sleep may have been difficult to get. The mental strain of their current situation far outweighed the physical strain she experienced, but at least the physical strain demanded sleep. And with sleep, she didn't have to think about how many friends she lost over the past few months.

None of this had been part of the plan. The exact opposite, actually. She had planned with Connor for months, trying to come up with a solution that wouldn't result in war. The last thing they wanted was to trigger a war, set off by a chain of events that would destroy more of the city and kill almost everyone they knew. She glanced at Connor, still sleeping opposite her. Even while he slept, she saw the pain and stress on his face.

Her head surged with pain and every heartbeat intensified the jabs that shot across her forehead. *Water.* Despite having plenty to drink and eat, she was dehydrated. She'd never been good at making herself drink enough and with all the walking they did, it only made it worse.

She fumbled for her flashlight, trying to minimize the noise. Sleep was a valuable commodity they all needed, and knowing Connor, the slightest noise would wake him up. He considered it his responsibility to keep them all safe and he couldn't do that successfully without a good night sleep. She didn't want to rob him of this much needed rest just so she could get a drink of water.

A soft cough drew her attention from her bag. Diesel grinned and waved her over. She pulled her water bottle out of the bag then fished around until she found the pain killers and a small snack. She turned in his direction. Diesel was not a person she liked. He was responsible for the death of her best friend and she never forgave him for it. He dealt drugs and had pushed them onto her friend who later died of a drug overdose. It was partly what got him banned from the Order and forced into the Levels years ago.

She shook her head and stepped back towards the wall where she had been sleeping. He dropped his grin and mouthed the word, *please*.

"I can't," she whispered.

"Sure you can." He pushed himself up to a seated position. "You don't have to say anything, just listen."

"I don't want to listen to anything you have to say." She dropped back down to the floor. She would have left if there had been somewhere to go, but she was stuck here and there was no escaping him.

"Well, I'm gonna talk whether you like it or not." He leaned his back against the wall behind him, grunting under his breath. "You never gave me a chance to explain—none of you."

"What was there to explain?" The harshness in her voice made him retract, which gave her an odd sense of joy. He was nervous to talk to her and it showed. She didn't even need her magic to tell her that.

"A lot if you'll let me." His eyes begged. The pain and torment he had to live with over his actions seeped from his expression. He suffered plenty and it made her smile. She didn't care. He deserved to feel bad, to beat himself up over what he did. "Who knows how much longer I have, at least give me a chance."

"You didn't deserve your fate." Her magic stirred and flames danced in her eyes. The anger she harbored towards him was insurmountable and he had a lot of nerve thinking she'd consider talking to him. "Life. That's the chance you were given. Your victims weren't given that chance. They're all dead. If it had been up to me, you wouldn't have gotten out of there alive."

"Kat, please."

"No!" Her voice escalated and her hands shook. Faint flames sparked in her fingertips. Any more of this and her magic would burst.

He flinched at the sight of her hands. He slumped back to his place on the floor, and she opened the bottle of medicine. He didn't bother saying anything else to her, which she was grateful for. A small part of her felt a little guilty for not giving him a chance. Life in the Levels had to be tough, and anyone sentenced to that place had it bad. Then again, her friend was dead and it was his fault.

CHAPTER TWENTY-ONE

2031: Day 79, Wednesday

They were all restless, especially Connor.

They'd been held up in the hidden storage closet for days, but it felt like weeks. Diesel slept most of the time, which was good, but his fever persisted and gave no sign of breaking. The antibiotics did nothing for him, and the outcome was not in his favor.

Katrina gave into rest often but insisted she was fine. Connor wanted her to rest longer and she argued to move on. He understood her underlying reason to keep moving—to get as far away from Diesel as possible. She was ready to leave him for dead. She knew from the onset where Connor was taking him. Diesel was the only person he knew who could do the surgery—and she knew that—but he also never intended for her to see him.

With no natural light able to penetrate the room or the long, rocky corridor outside, it was impossible for them to keep time. It was always dark and with nothing to do but stare at each other, time meant nothing. It was cramped, hot, and stuffy. It was a miserable state to be in.

Connor needed rest just as much as everyone else, but sleep was hard for him. The full weight of the city pressed down on him and the fate of Ebony and Charlotte was his to alter. He got them all in this mess and it was his responsibility to find a way to get them all out of it.

Everyone slept soundly when he tiptoed out the door and squeezed his way back to the streets. It was dark, the full moon high in the sky.

The streets were empty with no signs of security patrolling the area. He slipped around the corner to a section of the building that used to stand above them. The rubble was piled in a perfect, stair-like pattern, making it easy to climb to the top. Climbing up was the easy part. The roof, however, was pocketed with holes and sunken in areas. He'd made this climb every night the past two days to look around the city, and get some fresh air. Up there, the wind still blew, wiping away the stench that settled on all of them.

He settled in his seat at the top and gazed up at the stars. It was a clear night, and the lack of life and light in his surroundings made the stars shine brighter than ever. The lights from the surrounding areas of Manhattan that remained were too far away to pollute his view. Despite how much he hated the darkness, he couldn't help but smile at the beauty in the night sky tonight.

Most of Manhattan still stood and beamed with life. Magical Bond life. Behind him, opposite Manhattan, was a different view altogether.

He shifted his position away from Manhattan towards the river. It the Harlem River which joined with the East River just beyond the large island that separated them. Just past that was the tiny island that changed his life forever. The light of the moon sparkled on the water giving shape to the faint ripples. The reflection pushed back the shadows of darkness, but only slightly. Somewhere beyond the darkness was Research Island—the place he lost his best friend and Ebony remained in danger.

Hints of flickering light far in the distance caught his eye, and he thought maybe that was it. He let his mind pretend it was Research Island and Ebony slept safely behind the protection of its walls. Maybe Charlotte was there, too. If nothing else, it gave him a physical location to hold onto. It gave him a tangible goal and hope they were alive and waiting for him to rescue them.

The sound of falling rocks from the path he climbed minutes ago made him jump out of his seat. He crouched behind the edge of the half wall where he was sitting and waited. Feeling around in his pocket, he still had the small pocket knife he'd stashed there days before. It wasn't much, but it was better than nothing. Whoever decided to follow him up that wall was about to regret it.

For the first time in days, he allowed his magic to surface. He avoided using his magic since his run-in with those soldiers, only letting it surface in times of great need. Vivian and SUM could not be trusted, nor would he underestimate how far their technology had advanced. For all he knew, they created some crazy instrument to seek out magic wielders. He was being paranoid, but one could never be too safe.

He sent his magic out, twisting through the rubble and down the narrow rock stairway. *Katrina.* He relaxed and felt a little stupid for overreacting. *What's she doing following me?* She needed rest more than any of them and had no business being out this late—and certainly not climbing this death trap.

He sat back down on the half wall and waited for her to turn the last corner.

"What are you doing following me up here?" Connor said just before her face appeared. His eyes narrowed and his lips curled downward. "You should be sleeping."

"How much sleep do you think one person can get without losing their mind?" She shot him a crooked smile. Connor shook his head. She had no intention of listening to him and he knew he might as well give up trying to care for her. "I've had all the rest I can handle."

"But your injuries, they need more time." He turned his back to her and faced the river. He wanted to move in on SUM days ago, but he couldn't do this on his own. He needed her, all of them, if they hoped to succeed. Surely, she understood how important her recovery was to him. "You're no good to me weak. I need you to be at your best."

"Stop acting like my father. He's dead." She worked herself up next to him. He offered her a hand, but she refused. She couldn't hop up with ease as he did, but she still managed without too much difficulty. Maybe she was in better condition than he gave her credit. "If we keep delaying this rescue mission, we risk them being moved. For all we know Ebony and Charlotte are not on that island."

"I realize that, but we have to go in there ready for a tough fight." He held his eyes on hers. She didn't flinch or show the slightest hint of weakness. He nodded and pinched his lips together before he continued. "Are you saying you're at your best?"

"Are any of us at our best?" She held her chin high, a firm look in her eyes. "A few broken ribs don't affect my magic and my magic is at its peak. Delaying so I can rest isn't going to change anything."

"We don't have enough supplies. We're running low on everything." Connor glanced over his shoulder towards Manhattan. The hospital was several blocks in the opposite direction. Going back for more supplies would cost them a few days travel. "We have no idea what's in front of us and we can't leave here unprepared."

"I agree." She spoke with a confidence he'd never seen in her before. It pleased him to see how much she'd grown over these past few months, but he hated the events that triggered her growth. If he could go back and change the past, she never would have been exposed to Dr. Hunter, even if there was a positive outcome to his experimentation. Connor always knew she had the potential to be a strong, fierce leader and she was certainly showing him that side of her now. "In the morning, let's discuss it with the group. We do this together."

"Together." He looked at her out of the corner of his eye. He believed the words she spoke but doubted the team hidden deep within the half-crumbled walls they sat upon. Connor trusted Sullivan. He would do anything necessary to save his sister. But Diesel and Ajax were different matters. Diesel wasn't improving, and Ajax was a wild card. Connor didn't know anything about him and knew nothing about his magical ability. Ajax wasn't exactly forthcoming with knowledge either. Connor sensed his magic, knew it was strong, but couldn't figure out if he possessed special abilities like them. He suspected he did because of the way he blocked Connor's ability to read his mind. He feared that truth. No matter how angry it made Katrina, they needed to have a conversation about Ajax's magic before they planned their next move.

CHAPTER TWENTY-TWO

2031: Day 81, Friday

Connor was no more rested than he was two days ago. No matter his exhaustion, his mind would not calm and let his body rest. Last night had been worse than any night before. Diesel drew his last breath and left the world.

As soon as Connor saw the gray, pale color of his skin, he knew Diesel's end was near. Connor sat with him all night, whispering comforting words in his ear. He still sat with him, even though he passed hours ago. Another man lost to the war he started.

Connor nudged Sullivan, waking him from his deep sleep. Sullivan rolled over and looked him in the eyes. Connor held his finger to his mouth, leaned down and whispered. "Diesel, he...he's gone."

Sullivan shot up and glance down at Diesel's lifeless body. Connor was surprised by the sadness in Sullivan's eyes. Sullivan hadn't known Diesel long, but the time they spent together created a bond he hadn't sensed until now.

"Despite his shortcomings, he was a good man," Sullivan said.

"Yes...yes, he was." Connor nodded. "Will you help me get him out of here, give him a burial somewhere? Or at least a proper send-off."

Sullivan nodded and dropped his head in silence. Connor had never thought of Sullivan as a praying man, but he couldn't help but think he was praying for Diesel now.

Connor tip-toed towards the door and stepped outside. He sat his flashlight on the edge of a rock and turned it on, providing just enough light for them to get Diesel out without waking Katrina and Ajax. He saw no reason to wake either of them. Ajax didn't know Diesel, and Katrina would be happy at the news.

By the time Connor turned to pick up Diesel, Sullivan had already tossed him over his shoulder and carried him out the door. Together, they walked into the darkness to say goodbye to a friend.

BY THE TIME CONNOR AND SULLIVAN made their way back, the sun was rising. With Diesel gone, there was no reason to wait another day to plan their rescue. They still had a lot of details to work out. Finding a boat was important and may be challenging, but it was not his greatest concern. They had no way to confirm if Ebony was still on the island or if Charlotte had been taken there. Their only option was to go and search.

Connor opened the door and stopped, which made Sullivan bump into him and stub his toe.

"What?" Sullivan groaned.

"Ajax." Connor gritted his teeth. "He's gone."

Connor turned around, pushed his way past Sullivan, and raced down the corridor. Connor knew better than to trust Ajax. *The first moment we leave him alone with Katrina he takes off.* If Ajax double-crossed them, no man alive would be able to stop Connor from killing him. He had no clue which way he went or where to start looking, but he'd find him.

Connor had made the walk down the corridor so many times over the past few days, he knew every jagged edge and turn like the back of his hand. In a matter of minutes, he exited the other end and was standing in the middle of the flattened city.

Voices.

Connor ducked back into the passageway and hid behind a large boulder. There were soldiers just around the corner. Not once in the time they've hidden here had he seen a single soldier, and now a group was heading in his direction. His face warmed from his concentrated anger.

"Damn you, Ajax," Connor said under his breath. And damn himself for allowing Ajax to stay. His gut and his magic told him not to trust him, but he let it go for Katrina. He held his breath as the sounds of their voices grew closer—so close all they would have to do is look around the corner and they'd see him. He didn't have time to work his way further into the corridor without being caught. If he made the slightest sound, he'd be discovered. They paused on the other side of his hiding place.

"Any word on when we get to go home?" a gruff male voice asked.

"When it's done," said a woman with authority and a bit of disgust in her voice. "Stop asking questions and just keep your eyes open. They could be anywhere."

"It'd help if we knew who we were looking for," a second man said. Connor let a tiny bit of his magic slip free so he could sense their minds. There were four of them, and he couldn't take four trained soldiers by himself if he was discovered. He held his breath and hoped their presence was a coincidence.

"Irrelevant. We see anyone, it doesn't matter who they are, we take them in." The woman spoke again. He heard the frustration in her voice. She was in charge of these three and didn't care for them. Connor sensed that much from her. "Keep quiet. You all talk too much. If there is anyone around here, they heard us coming a mile away. Let's move."

They moved on. The men continued to talk despite the order from their leader, either from lack of respect or just plain stupidity. Either way, Connor waited and listened until their chatter disappeared then he headed back down the corridor towards the hidden room.

Maybe those soldiers showed up outside their hiding place because Ajax gave away their location. Maybe Ajax did nothing and those soldiers were idiots. Regardless, Connor wanted him gone and hoped he never returned. Connor's magic didn't trust him and no matter how many times he tried to get a reading on Ajax, he couldn't penetrate his mind. One thing was for certain, if Ajax returned, he better have a great reason why he disappeared in the first place.

CONNOR SLAMMED THE DOOR OPEN, his eyes wild. Katrina was awake and sitting next to Sullivan. Connor grabbed her by the shoulders and pulled her up until her face was level with his. "Where is he?" he growled.

"I don't know, probably scavenging for supplies." Katrina's voice was calm, but a bright, red flame danced in her eyes. "That's what he does best. Or have you not been listening?"

"He should be here." Connor let her go and took in a deep breath. Katrina stood firm in her place and held her gaze on him. Her anger towards him was strong and he sensed her magic building for an attack. "Are you going to fight me?"

"No." She shook her head and laughed. "That would be pointless. But I am pissed at you. I'm not the same person I was six months ago. I'm stronger, more powerful than ever, and all you want to do is treat me like a child."

Connor stepped back and watched her closely. Despite her anger towards him, she controlled her emotions and maintained a calmness he'd rarely seen in another. Katrina had always been more mellow than the other members of the Order, but this was different. She had changed.

"Ajax shouldn't have left," Connor yelled. "We need to stay together, that's the only way we can keep each other safe."

"I don't recall a ban on anyone leaving this room." Katrina looked to Sullivan and shrugged. "I don't understand why you're freaking out so much. Am I missing something?"

Connor leaned against the wall opposite Katrina and dropped his head. Stress, lack of sleep, and constant worry were tearing him apart. He slowed his breathing and centered his mind. Losing his temper with her wouldn't do any good. He had to calm down and remain rational.

"What do you know about Ajax?" Connor asked.

"I told you already. He pulled me out of the rubble after the explosion. He's from the Brooklyn North outpost." Despite the calmness in her voice, her face was red with anger. "Why are you so angry at me."

"I'm not angry at you, I'm angry at myself." Connor dropped to the floor. Every ounce of energy he had was gone. These past few months had been the most challenging of his life. He knew this was going to be tough. It was a near impossible feat to beat SUM and take down the government, but he had been determined to do it no matter the cost. He was wrong. He was not prepared and couldn't stand himself for the cost he'd already paid for the mission.

"Relax, Connor." Katrina spoke with authority. "We've been cooped up here for days. Ajax probably needed some fresh air. No different than when you sneak off in the middle of the night and you think the rest of us are sleeping."

Katrina paused in the doorway and glanced back at Connor. He looked up and met her stare, the flames in her eyes fading. "Take a moment and morn Diesel, then get some sleep. You look like shit and you're not acting much better."

Katrina left before Connor could respond. He started after her but decided to let her go. The soldiers he heard had moved on and she was smart enough not to get caught. She had never been so bold with him before and just then, she handled him. She proved to him he didn't have to take on the full weight of their situation alone. She was capable of helping him and maybe even succeeding where he failed. It was time he relaxed and let her do more of the leading. Maybe then he'd get some rest.

THE LOW WHISPER OF VOICES STIRRED Connor from his deep sleep. Several lanterns were lit, more than Connor thought they had, making the room bright as daylight.

He sat up, blinking several times forcing his eyes to adjust. Sullivan was organizing their supplies and repacking their backpacks. This final mission would end it all, one way or another, succeed or fail. This was it, and there would be no third chances. If they failed it could end their lives and any momentum this rebellion had. But if they succeeded, they could handicap SUM, turning the tables and shifting the advantage in their direction. The stark difference between the two possible outcomes made Connor sick to his stomach. Win and they save the people. Lose and the people would be enslaved indefinitely. Then again, was there really such a thing as indefinite where war was concerned? If they lost this war, someone else would rise in his place and succeed where he failed. People only take oppression and abuse so long before they rise against the oppressor. If he failed, someone stronger, braver, would rise and win. He had to believe that.

"How long did I sleep?" Connor asked.

"Several hours, maybe six or seven. It's late afternoon." Sullivan patted him on the shoulder and grinned.

Six or seven hours? He dropped his head in his hands and sighed. Too much time was wasted. They should have had their plan worked out and on their way to the river by now. A Saturday attack was their best bet. Fewer employees would be working, and Dr. Hunter never worked on Saturdays. He often disappeared on Saturdays, and Connor hoped he maintained that same routine. "Where's Kat?"

Sullivan pointed towards the open door. Katrina stood close to Ajax, her arms wrapped around his waist and his arm hugged her shoulder. A strong urge called Connor to separate them. The sight of them holding each other set off his defenses and every warning signal. They stood over an open flame with a large pot.

Connor shuffled to his feet, grabbing Katrina's attention. She pulled herself away from Ajax and poured a drink in a mug.

"Here." Katrina walked into the room and handed him a steaming mug.

"What's this?" Connor let the steam from the mug wash over his face as he inhaled the rich aroma of coffee.

Katrina crossed her arms over her chest. Ajax paused and stared at her. "While you were busy accusing Ajax of betrayal, he was off scouting a path and gathering supplies. In case you hadn't noticed, we were getting dangerously close to running out of water. You have him to thank for the coffee."

"But." Connor paused and stared at Katrina with questioning eyes.

"I told you, he's a great scavenger." Katrina turned back to Ajax and leaned against his side.

Connor swallowed hard. His lengthy nap helped clear his mind, but his anger and mistrust of Ajax remained strong. He forced a smile and for the first time since meeting Ajax, addressed him directly. "Hot coffee? How did you manage that one?"

"Chafing fuel from a catering business close by. They had tons of it and water. Food, too." Ajax pointed to the row of boxes lined up against the wall. "It took several trips to bring that here, but it should last us a while if we need it."

Connor leaned forward and looked around the corner. At least ten boxes, maybe more, lined the wall. He relaxed his shoulders and let his back fall against the wall behind him.

"Hungry?" Ajax asked. "I'm making chili."

"All right." Connor took a sip of his coffee and turned his back to Ajax. It was hot and strong, just the way he liked it. With any luck, it would give him the energy boost he needed to get through the next two days. Getting on Research Island would be easy, but getting back off with Ebony and Charlotte was a different story. Connor was grateful for the coffee and food Ajax found, but it would take a hell of a lot more than coffee to earn his trust. He glanced up and caught Katrina glaring at him. "What?"

"Seriously." Her voice cracked. "Come on, Connor. Why is that so hard for you?"

Connor's lips tightened when Katrina reached over and squeezed Ajax's hand. There was more than trust in that squeeze. There was a mutual attraction and bond between them, one he tried to deny existed despite how close he'd seen them get these past few days. If Ajax was working against them, she wouldn't see it if he acted against them right in front of her. Her sight was blinded by her feelings for him. Those feelings put Connor in a tough position. He had no choice but to accept Ajax or else risk losing Katrina. Right or wrong, she was falling for this stranger and if he continued to push the issue, she would leave. Connor couldn't afford to lose Katrina, too.

"Fine," he sighed. "Thanks, Ajax. Much appreciated."

Ajax nodded and went back to cooking. At least he knew when to keep his mouth shut. Connor would give him that. Katrina on the other hand, she kept talking.

"He also found us a boat and a clear path to the river," Katrina said with her back towards him. "Now that we have transportation, we need a plan. Do you think you can handle that one, Connor?"

Now she was trying to piss him off. He gritted his teeth, biting the inside of his cheek to keep from firing back at her. This wasn't the time for a fight and she knew that. She knew how hard all this was for him, yet she pushed his buttons anyway. He was leery of Ajax for a good reason, and she of all people should respect that.

He let her last remark go. Responding would only make it worse. Instead, he grabbed a pointy rock that he could use for drawing on the dust covered floor and drew a layout of the island.

CHAPTER TWENTY-THREE

2031: Day 81, Late Friday

The full layout of Research Island covered the floor before them. Connor drew every building, walkway, and structure he remembered. He labeled each building and wrote little notes on his discoveries in the dirt with a stick. Chances were, nothing much had changed. His stick writing was hard to read, but he wanted everyone to know where to go and where to avoid.

Connor studied what he drew, pleased with all he remembered. He made a few more notes in the dirt and called the others over.

"We land here." Connor pointed to the edge of the island next to the lighthouse. "There's no dock and it's mostly rocks. We may have to wade through the water's edge to get to shore, but it's the safest place to land."

"Dr. Hunter might be expecting that," Katrina said. "He knows that's where we hid and planned our escape. What if it's guarded?"

"I thought about that." That was exactly what Connor would do if he was in charge of protecting the island. He'd have the lighthouse constantly on surveillance. But SUM security wasn't him and neither was Dr. Hunter. Dr. Hunter's arrogance was Connor's advantage. That arrogance would give them a way in. "Yes, it's a possibility, but I don't think so. As we get close to shore, Sully will use his power to makes us all invisible. I'll use my magic to sense for warm bodies. Assuming the lighthouse is empty, we dock and hide out in the ground-floor room until we make our move."

"And what if there are warm bodies?" Sullivan asked.

"If the lighthouse is guarded, our next best bet is to land over here." Connor pointed to the edge of the island on the eastern side near the compound. "There are enough trees to give us cover and keep the boat out of sight while we find Ebony and Charlotte."

"Why not just go there and avoid this lighthouse altogether," Ajax asked. "I realize I've never been there but if there's a chance they'd expect us there we should avoid it."

Connor watched Ajax closely. This was the most he'd spoken to him since he showed up with Katrina. His silence had given Connor further reason to mistrust him. Connor didn't hear the nervousness in his voice but he saw it in his hands when he pointed at the map. Connor couldn't hold back the smile that crept across his face.

"The problem with this location near the compound is it's also close to the security wing. There will be guards all over the place. I'd like to avoid using my magic for as long as possible. We have to assume Dr. Hunter has trained all his security to spot our magic, to know when one of them is under my control. The lighthouse is abandoned and as far away from the main operations of SUM as a building can be on the island. Despite what we did there before we left, I still think it's the safest bet."

Connor glanced around the group, briefly making eye contact with each one. No one objected to his reasoning, and he saw nothing but trust in their eyes. *Good.* He still had their trust as their leader despite his many mistakes.

"As we near the island," Connor looked to Sullivan, "do you think you can make us invisible, boat and all?"

"Yeah, that's easy," Sullivan answered.

Connor nodded. He really didn't have to ask Sullivan that question. Sullivan's magic was strong and he made a full recovery from the surgery to remove the tracker. Not much could hold Sullivan back now. As soon as he started testing his limits, he figured out his limits were high. Without effort, Sullivan could make this entire room and everyone in it disappear in seconds with the slightest touch of his hand. Even better, it resulted in minimal draining of his well. All of them, once they let themselves go to their magic, discovered a strength they never knew they possessed. The mission Connor set out to achieve may have been a complete failure, but they learned so much more about themselves, their magic, and the full extent they could push themselves. With their enhancement came power beyond one's imagination. To save his people, all he had to do was steal that power from SUM and use it for good. Sounds simple enough, but the hurdles before him were high.

"Once we land near the lighthouse, we'll need to scan from the top, confirm nothing has changed. Other than that, we hideout in the lower room until I locate Ebony and Char. I suspect Dr. Hunter is keeping them in one of three places. The main compound is always a possibility, but I think this building, where Ebony's mother was encapsulated, or where they inserted that sensor in Sully, is more likely." Connor pointed at each potential location as he spoke. He held his eyes on the building he drew to represent the location where the dissected and half mutilated bodies were found. Ebony and Charlotte were far too valuable to be cut up and used for parts. Dr. Hunter needed them alive to carry out his vision for SUM. At least that's what Connor tried to convince himself was true.

"Sully will go with me," Connor continued. "I'll need his power of invisibility to get in and out unseen. Kat, you and Ajax will stand guard, send us warnings should things get ugly out there."

"Warnings?" Ajax asked, the word he spoke barely audible. "Like what?"

"Magic. If danger arises, Kat will use magic to communicate with us." Connor spoke with confidence. "If Kat sends out a magical warning, we'll sense it. We may not know exactly what's going on, but we'll know to be on high alert and alter our path."

"Magic can do that?" Ajax's jaw dropped and his eyes widened.

"Yeah." Connor watched him closely. "My magic can sense danger, read minds, and even control others' motor skills. Except you. I haven't been able to get a read on you since we met. What are your magical abilities?"

"It's just magic." Ajax shrugged his shoulders. "Not much to tell."

"Then how are you blocking me?" Connor stood and crossed his arms over his chest.

"I didn't know I was." Ajax didn't move and gave no indication of feeling threated by Connor.

"That's enough, Connor." Katrina stepped in front of Ajax, separating him from Connor. "We have more important things to worry about right now. Time is running short. Can we get back to the plan?"

Connor slowly shifted his stare from Ajax to Katrina. He

wanted to object to her request and continue questioning Ajax. But the look in her eyes told him if he did, he'd have a real fight on his hands. While Connor was concerned about not being able to read Ajax, he couldn't deny Katrina was right. Any more delays and they may never find Ebony and Charlotte again. For all he knew, it was already too late.

"Fine," Connor said. "As I was saying, use your magic to warn us if danger heads our way."

"Do we stay at the lighthouse or follow you guys?" Ajax asked. "I mean, I don't want to get captured and following you seems dangerous."

"We'll follow to an extent," Katrina answered, pointing to an area on Connor's map close to the buildings. Connor dropped his head to hide his smile. He was glad she let the conversation continue. "There's a line of trees and bushes here. We can hide here unseen and watch for danger. We can see both these buildings without obstruction. If they're in the main compound, then that's a different story."

"If they're in the main compound, then take the path that loops around the southern edge of the island and hide out in this area. The trees are thick there." Connor pointed at the alternative landing location, near the security wing. He looked up at Katrina, whose expression was covered in doubt and fear. "Am I missing something?"

"Well, I've been wondering. More concerned really," she said. "What if our magic doesn't work?"

"It'll work. Ban or no ban, there's no known substance to hinder magic wielding." Connor didn't hesitate in his response.

"Yeah, but..."

"It'll work." Connor cut her off. *It had to work.* "Once I locate them, Sully and I will collect them and meet you two back at the boat. Keep your distance, stay hidden, but keep an eye on us. Use your magic to clear a path for us if necessary. If all goes to plan, we'll be in and out in less than thirty minutes."

Connor glanced between the three of them to get a read on their expressions. They all had looks of concern and doubt. "Any questions."

Everyone shook their heads no. Connor nodded in response and maintained his confidence in their success. He'd never admit it, but he too was worried about their magic working. Without magic, they'd fail and end up captured. They had the element of surprise in their favor. No one was expecting them, but without magic, they'd be vulnerable and unable to locate Ebony and Charlotte. He pushed the thought out of his mind and held onto the hope their magic would work. It had to work. All hope of success hinged on his magic reaching Ebony and Charlotte. His power was strong and nothing would stop him from finding his friends. He knew their spirit, their magical essence, and more importantly, his magic knew them. He'd find them, and nothing would stop that power.

CHAPTER TWENTY-FOUR

2031: Day 82, Early Saturday

The night air was cold, and the wind brought with it a wet blanket that sent a chill through Katrina's body. Summer was at an end and fall was taking root. The boat Ajax found for them was small and provided no protection from the elements. They had to take turns rowing the boat across the river and everyone's tired arms made it slow moving. At this rate, they'd freeze to death before they reached the island without a little magical help, and Katrina was just the one to provide it.

Katrina's control over fire could provide enough heat to keep them all warm. Assuming she didn't let it escape her grasp and burn a hole in the boat, everyone would be fine. She drew deep within and called upon the fire inside her, pulling out the heat, but suppressing the flame itself. Separating her magic like this was easy on small scales, but this open space made it much harder. The flame fought hard to escape her grasp.

A faint glow hovered just above the surface of her skin, but there were no flames. She pushed the heat outward, away from her body, and the glow spread until it surrounded the entire boat and everyone in it.

"Katrina!" Connor looked amazed and confused. "Since when could you do this?"

"I did this on a small scale before Ajax and I found you." She smiled. "I'm freezing, assumed you all were too. I figure actual flames would be a bit much, so I pulled the heat out to share with all of you."

The group went from shivering and miserable, to calm and comfortable in a matter of seconds. This probably was the most comfortable any of them had been in days. Everyone slouched back and relaxed. It'd take another thirty minutes or more before they docked near the lighthouse and her heat was a welcomed luxury.

Their journey through the city to the boat was much easier than any of them anticipated and they reached the boat in record time. Ajax led the way via a route he scouted out during the hours he disappeared. Even Katrina couldn't deny the oddity of that. He swore they wouldn't see a single soldier, and he was right. It was too easy. So easy, it worried Katrina. Ajax was a good man, she had no doubt of that, he'd saved her life when he could have left her to die. She would never forget all he'd done for her, but the ease of the journey was alarming.

She kept an eye on Ajax, unable to get Connor's voice out of her mind. Ajax remained quiet most of the journey, only speaking when he needed to tell them which direction to go. Even now he looked relaxed, his legs stretched out in front of him and his hands locked behind his head. He caught her staring at him and smiled. She smiled back before she dropped her head. She felt foolish. Foolish for staring at him like a school girl with a crush and foolish for questioning his loyalty at the same time. She refused to let Connor's paranoia and lack of trust in others suck her into his world of misery.

Yes, misery. Connor Vance was miserable and in some ways, he wanted everyone around him to be miserable, too. She refused to let his misery infiltrate her mind and sway her life decisions. He hadn't always been this way, he used to be full of life and welcoming to all who wanted to join the Order's cause. But this past year took a lot of out him, particularly this past month. Even now, she could see the stress in his eyes; his tired and worried eyes. If all went as planned, this would end today, and they could begin to rebuild their lives in the wake of this war. There would certainly be more fighting to endure but succeeding at saving Ebony and Charlotte was a huge step in the right direction. Life was too short for this constant fear and mistrust in those around her. She refused to let this become her destiny.

With her magical warmth, the remainder of the trip across the river passed quickly, and they docked the boat in the shadow of the lighthouse. Connor motioned for them all to stay put while he surveyed the area with his magic.

"There's no one here." He motioned for them to follow him to the lighthouse.

Katrina stood at the edge of the boat and hesitated to take that last step off. She'd never planned on coming back to this place, ever. A chill ran through her bones, snuffing out all the warmth she stored inside her. This island was evil, and her magic warned her to run, to turn around and go the other direction. She wanted to obey her magical spirit that guided and protected her, but she had to help save her friends. *I must.* She silently called out to her magic. *I must take this step.*

Her body worked against her when she lifted her foot over the boat. Her magic pulled her back, doing its best to keep her off the island. It weighed her down, making it difficult to breathe.

"Are you okay?" Ajax stood behind her, a worried look on his face.

"Yeah," she whispered. She looked past the lighthouse to the grouping of buildings near the center. "Let's get this over with and get out of here."

A memory of the last time she stood in this spot surfaced in her mind. The image of Sullivan on the ground, his body twitching, made her cringe. That was also the day Connor disappeared. He was taken and beaten by Dr. Hunter. If Dr. Hunter had his way, none of them would leave this island alive. She forced the memory and her fear for all their lives out of her mind. She focused on taking one step at a time.

By the time she entered the ground floor room of the lighthouse, Connor was coming back down the stairs.

"Everything looks the same." Connor was out of breath. He was too tired from the lack of sleep. They all were. "No guards anywhere near us either. I only spotted two near the edge of the path by the compound. Hopefully, most of the path will be clear."

"Could you sense Char?" Sully asked, his body tense.

"I haven't searched yet." Connor squeezed Sullivan's shoulder. "Don't worry, we'll find them."

Connor sat on the floor near the wall and crossed his legs. With his eyes closed, he took in several deep breaths.

Katrina leaned against the opposite wall and warmed the room. Might as well make this place as comfortable as possible while they waited. Now that they were here, worry filled her mind and her magic would not calm no matter how much she tugged it back. They'd put too much hope in Connor finding Ebony and Charlotte with his magic and didn't bother to come up with a backup plan. Would they really go blindly into one of these buildings if Connor didn't sense one of them? That sounded like the stupidest idea Katrina could think of.

But what other options did they have?

Leaving Charlotte and Ebony in the hands of SUM was not an option any of them could live with. They had to get them back. *Connor will find them.* Katrina did her best to convince herself that was true even though deep down she questioned the possibility.

The look on Sullivan's face said the same thing. He too was trying to stay calm, but his eyes said he was ready to tear apart whoever stepped in his way and tried to keep him away from his sister. Katrina took a step towards Sullivan, but Connor shot up and was on his feet before she lifted her other foot.

"I found Char!" Connor sprinted to the door and opened it. "Let's go before we lose the cover of darkness."

CHAPTER TWENTY-FIVE

2031: Day 82, Early Saturday

Sullivan ran after Connor, knocking Ajax down. Katrina grimaced at the sound of the loud crunch his hip made when he hit the ground. She called out for Connor to wait but he was out the door, Sullivan right behind him, completely disregarding the plan they discussed. They were going to get them all caught if they didn't slow down and think before they went flying across the island.

"Are you okay?" Katrina held out her hand and helped Ajax up.

"I'm fine." He smiled and wiped the dirt from his pants. He reached out and brushed his fingertips across her cheek and she blushed. She held his stare, only dropping her eyes when he made a move towards her. She sensed his desire to kiss her and hold her in a deep embrace. She wanted it, too. Stepping forward, she wrapped her arms around his neck and met his lips before he had a chance to fully act on his desires.

There was no way of knowing how this rescue mission

was going to turn out and, selfish or not, she was going to feel his lips on hers one last time. He welcomed every inch of her into his embrace. She melted under his touch and if her magic hadn't tugged at her she would've lost herself completely in his kiss.

"We better go before Sully and Connor make it halfway across the island." Katrina wrapped her arms tight around his neck and held him close for a moment before she pushed away. She met his eyes and smiled. The ravishing look on his face nearly pulled her back into his lips, but she resisted. "This will have to wait."

She took one step towards the open door and froze. Connor and Sullivan stood motionless before her. Connor glanced her way and with the slightest movement of his eyes, he told her to stay. She hesitated, not sure if she should obey or run out to see what they faced.

"What's wrong?" Ajax whispered in her ear.

"Not sure, but Connor says to stay inside." She stepped back, guiding the door until it closed silently. She ran to the window on the opposite wall, still covered with the paper Ebony taped over it weeks ago. Ajax helped her peel it away revealing the army of SUM security surrounding the lighthouse. Katrina guessed there had to be at least fifty men, maybe more, blocking their path. Dressed in black suits and hats, the darkness of night shielded their true numbers, but she could tell they were all armed with guns aimed in the direction of Connor and Sullivan.

Katrina didn't hesitate or think. There was no way she was going to stay in here and leave Connor to face them alone. They were in this together no matter the outcome. She ran out the door and skidded to a stop behind Connor. Sullivan was kneeling on the ground, his head down and his body shaking. Katrina couldn't tell if he was hurt or trying to regain control of his emotions. He lifted his head and the look in his eyes aside these past few days and focus on her strength, but the emotional scars from his mental rape of her magic were too close to the surface, and her magic grew beyond her control.

Sullivan shot forward, propelling himself directly at Dr. Hunter, but an invisible force knocked him down flat on his back. He tried to get up, but he couldn't. His body was trapped, pressed down by an invisible weight. He gasped for air, struggling to breathe.

"Sully!" Katrina snapped back and ran to Sullivan's side. She pulled at his arms, but his body wouldn't move. The harder she pulled up, the wider his eyes. With every pull, the magical weight pressed harder against his chest, cutting off his air supply.

Katrina looked to Connor for help, but he didn't run to Sullivan's aid. Connor didn't even bother to turn and look at his friend. Instead, he ran forward, blasting a wave of his own magic towards Dr. Hunter. His blast broke through the invisible wall, sending sparks of blue light in every direction, and hitting Dr. Hunter in the chest. Dr. Hunter fell backward, disappearing into the army of security guards. Sullivan was instantly released from the magical weight that pressed down on him. He struggled to stay upright as he recovered from the loss of oxygen.

Katrina helped Sullivan up, relieved he was all right. He gasped for air and looked terrified by the magic that held him down. Katrina had never seen magic like that, and her magic gave her no warning of its presence. Either Dr. Hunter created more enhanced Magical Bond that produced an invisible wall, or he'd successfully manipulated his own magic to be equally as powerful as theirs.

A bright, blue light flashed and blinded Katrina. Connor stepped forward, his body surrounded by a magical force field. His magic had grown, too. Light had never manifested from his magic before. Even he looked surprised by the form his told her everything she needed to know.

The rage of a wild lion ready for battle consumed his face.

A golden flicker danced around Sullivan's pupils and his growl sang out the battle cry. Katrina followed his stare and saw the true source of his rage. It wasn't the army surrounding them.

At the front of the line in his usual white lab coat stood Dr. Daniel Hunter, the man who created them for evil and abused his own daughter for years to advance his research. Anger fed Katrina's magic, same as it was doing to Sullivan. Her magic sparked and concentrated in her hands, ready to attack the man responsible for bombing half the city and killing most of their friends. She thought she was prepared to face him again, but she was wrong. He stood before them, smiling and proud in his crisp, white lab coat, which only fueled her anger more.

Katina's magic swarmed around her, spreading its way between them and Dr. Hunter. Excitement danced in his eyes. He was prepared for their return. She took a step back, every ounce of her body and magic telling her to run, but she couldn't leave her friends behind.

Katrina's skin crawled with disgust, and she recoiled. Her involuntary response drew Dr. Hunter's eyes to her. "Hello, Miss Hicks. So good to see you've continued our lessons and finally gave into your strength."

He stared in awe at the flames that formed from her hands. She squeezed her hands into fists and the flames shot downward, skipping across the ground until they burned out. She was losing control over her magic. Seeing Dr. Hunter, smug and proud, was harder than she expected it to be. She knew who this man was, but nothing prepared her for the emotions that consumed her. Seeing him again triggered the memories of her last training session with him, when he invaded her body. She managed to push those memories magic took.

She caught the look in Connor's eyes a moment too late. Before she could yell at him to stop, he crashed into the guards knocking the closest ones to the ground. Dr. Hunter stood before him with his arms stretched open as if to welcome home a lost child.

Connor sent another blast of his magic at Dr. Hunter, only this time nothing happened despite the direct hit in the chest. Dr. Hunter's body never so much as twitched at the blast from Connor. The look in Dr. Hunter's eyes sent a chill down Katrina's spine. *He's playing with us.* Everything they planned was futile. None of it mattered. Dr. Hunter had been prepared for them as if he knew their every move before they did.

The glow surrounding Connor brightened, and Katrina squinted. He drew deeper, calling upon every ounce of his power and sent another blast of magic at Dr. Hunter, this time aiming for his head. Katrina couldn't believe what she saw. Nothing Connor did made a dent in Dr. Hunter. His magic bounced off him, never so much as causing the slightest discomfort or pain. Dr. Hunter took a step closer to Connor and laughed.

Katrina's legs weakened and she started to fall. The disbelief over the strength of magic resisting Connor overwhelmed her, and the strength of her magic overpowered her mind. She grabbed Sullivan's hand for support. Unlike her, Sullivan's face showed no signs of fear. Instead, he looked ready to pounce on Dr. Hunter and join Connor in this magical battle.

She held tight to Sullivan's hand and leaned against his shoulder. He glanced at her, and his face softened. He stepped back and leaned into her, providing the support she needed in this moment. His magic redirected towards her, feeding her strength and giving her energy the boost it needed. Katrina held up her free hand and wielded her magic into concentrated balls of fire. She drew only what she needed from Sullivan to push all her fear aside and regain control of her magic. Concentrated balls of fire shot past Connor and cut through the guards, knocking them to the ground. Dr. Hunter stumbled but recovered before he fell. He smiled at her and stepped forward.

"Did you learn nothing from our last encounter?" Dr. Hunter said before he stopped in front of Connor. "You cannot beat your creator."

Connor drew his fist back and threw a punch at Dr. Hunter's face, but the invisible force that knocked Sullivan to the ground stopped his fist inches from Dr. Hunter's cheek. Laughter escaped the man before them. Connor tried to pull his fist back, but he was frozen the same way Sullivan had been frozen moments ago.

Dr. Hunter slowly walked around Connor, his eyes fixed on his face. "You're a fool, Connor. You never should've come back here, but I'm glad you did. Saves me the trouble of hunting you down."

With a slight flick of his hand, Dr. Hunter signaled one of the guards. The guard aimed and shot his gun at Connor, hitting him in the thigh. The power that held Connor motionless released him and he fell to the ground.

"No," Katrina yelled. She ran towards Connor, but the invisible wall stopped her. She screamed and banged at the air, each thrust of her fist blocked by the new power.

Connor grabbed his leg where he was shot and wrapped his hand around a tranquilizer needle. It was all he could do to pull it out before the drug took effect and he collapsed to the ground.

Katrina fell to her knees, tears running down her face. This couldn't be happening. This wasn't how it was supposed to go. They came here to save Ebony and Charlotte, not lose another friend. Katrina glared up at Dr. Hunter; her anger fueled by the smile on his face as the guards dragged Connor away.

"You'll never win," she yelled, her body turning red from the magic that grew within. She dragged her feet underneath her and pushed up to a standing position. She held nothing back, showed no restraint as her magic swelled. Everything within her shot out, covering every inch of ground before her. The invisible wall shattered, sending faint sparks into the air. Every guard fell, even Dr. Hunter was knocked over by her fiery blast.

"Well, that was unexpected." Dr. Hunter brushed off his pants as he stood back up. "I underestimated your strength, Katrina. I can't wait to harness that power."

"You'll never control me." She put up her own wall of protection, surrounding Sullivan within as well. Unlike Dr. Hunter's invisible force fields, hers flickered in flames. Shades of red and orange burned across every inch of the large dome that protected them from Dr. Hunter and his army of soldiers. Nothing would get through—she'd make sure of that.

Dr. Hunter lifted his hand and the guards hustled to their feet, reforming their line. They readied their weapons, waiting for the signal. The ones dragging Connor hadn't waited for an order and had already pulled him halfway across the path towards the buildings in the center of the island. She had to stop those guards before it was too late. She didn't have Connor's mental power to find him if she lost sight of him.

"Last chance, Katrina." Dr. Hunter never took his eyes off her. "Surrender and live, or fight and die."

"I'll never surrender." She stepped in front of Sullivan extending her flaming shield between them.

With a swift movement, Dr. Hunter dropped his hand. Every guard with a weapon drawn fired at Katrina. She held her position and steadied her hands in front of her. With all her strength, she pushed a wall of flames towards the guards. Dr. Hunter had been ready and prepared his own wall to protect his guards from her fire, but he didn't protect the tranquilizers flying in the air at her and Sullivan. Every needle fizzled in flames and fell to the ground.

Again Dr. Hunter lifted his hand and again the guards obeyed his orders. The result was the same. Her magic strengthened with each blast, her well continuously replenished. A gift she had been given. Maggy's endless well, now lived within each of them thanks to Ebony.

"I'm impressed with your growth." Dr. Hunter stepped up close to her wall of flames and ran his fingers over the surface. After a couple seconds, he drew his fingers back. "The heat is remarkable. If unleashed, I'd wager you could burn down every structure on this island."

"I'll only burn you." She increased the reach of her firewall, forcing him to step back. She glanced towards the lighthouse. Ajax was safely inside the doorway and out of harm's way.

Dr. Hunter shifted his stare in the direction she looked. "No, I'm afraid you won't." Dr. Hunter stepped towards the lighthouse and stopped a few feet shy of her firewall. "I see you've met Ajax."

She faltered. Searching the lighthouse, she found Ajax's eyes. They changed and no longer looked at her with affection and concern. His stare matched Dr. Hunter's sinister intent. Ajax shrugged and stepped around her barrier, stopping next to Dr. Hunter. This couldn't be happening. He loved her. That much she knew for certain.

"What are you doing?" A faint cry escaped her lips.

"Sorry, Kat." Ajax smiled and put his arm around Dr. Hunter's shoulder. "You really should learn to listen to your friends and not trust strangers."

"Excellent job, my son." Dr. Hunter patted him on the

back. "I didn't believe you would be able to convince them all to trust you, but you succeeded."

"I only had to win over one of them." Ajax held Katrina's stare. "She did all the hard work for me."

Katrina's eyes turned red first, followed by flames dancing around her face. Pain fed her power. Tears escaped her eyes, but the heat from the flames evaporated them before they made it down her cheeks. She wanted to scream at him, beg him to tell her it wasn't true, but shock kept her silent. She had been so certain everything he did for her was genuine, she felt it and her magic sensed it in him. Her magic had never failed her before, but he had found a way to trick it, to draw her magic to him.

"Don't be so hard on yourself, Kat. You didn't stand a chance against me." A smirk crept across Ajax's face.

His words turned her pain to anger and she centered her power in her chest. She showed no restraint. A solid beam of fire shot out of her chest hitting Ajax, and knocking him flat on his back.

"Wow." Ajax laughed so hard, and her anger flared more. Dark clouds rolled in, covering the rising sun. For the first time, Katrina let her elemental power expand to the atmosphere and draw out the electricity. A loud crack and a bright beam of lightning opened the ground at Ajax's feet.

"You will die today," Katrina growled, her voice unrecognizable. All reason left her. She didn't care what it took, even if it meant sacrificing herself.

"Katrina." Sullivan's voice called from behind. "We'd better get out of here." Sullivan's voice drew her eyes over her shoulder. He stared past her, towards Dr. Hunter. She followed his eyes and saw a swarm of guards heading towards them. Their numbers multiplied and a solid wall of guards separated them from the center of the island. The guards dragging Connor away were out of sight. Connor was gone, and she would not be finding him today.

Her magic had one objective, destroy everyone and everything in her path. Sullivan continued to yell at her, but her magic blocked the words and she couldn't make out what he said. It wasn't until he wrapped his arms around her and dragged her to the water's edge that she snapped out of it. She had been so consumed by revenge; she didn't recognize the danger they faced. If they didn't leave this island now, they too would be taken like Connor.

Katrina fought to pull her magic in and regain control. They failed at saving Ebony and Char, and now they lost Connor. There was nothing they could do to change that. There were too many guards for them to fight. Leaving and finding another way was their only option. She refused to let Sullivan or herself meet the same fate, but she wasn't finished with Dr. Hunter. Not yet.

Lightning struck all around them, lighting up the sky. Flashes of light reflected off Dr. Hunter's eyes and for a split second, she saw fear on his face. That fear gave her strength; strength to bring on a thunderous storm. The lightning intensified and deafening thunder rumbled from above. Heavy rain fell from the skies, with droplets so large and powerful they cut open the skin of all those they hit.

She returned Ajax's sinister smile when he attempted to shield his face from the rain only to have his shirt ripped open from the force of the water. Small gashes covered his skin and his blood joined the water responsible for the cuts. Ajax fell to the ground, curled into a ball attempting to shield himself from her wrath. Dr. Hunter stood next to Ajax and watched Katrina in awe. Not a single drop of her powerful rain made it to his skin. His own shield surrounded him and protected him from her magic.

"Come, my child." Dr. Hunter reached out for her hand.

"Let me teach you how to harness that power for a purpose."

The audacity of his words strengthened her hold on her power. She gathered the rain into a wall, replacing her wall of flames with water. The wall grew thicker with every drop of rain it intercepted, forcing Dr. Hunter and his guards to step back or be consumed by it. Within seconds, the wall grew too thick to see through, fading Dr. Hunter and his men from view.

"Katrina, we need to go, now." Sullivan wrapped his arms around her waist and dragged her to the boat. She fought her way free of him, holding her magic. Katrina stretched her arms up to the sky. Flashes of light gathered and concentrated in a swirl of electricity. With all the power within her, she clapped her hands together and the lightning struck, sending a bright bolt at the mass of guards on the other side of her wall of water. Bodies ran in every direction, burning from the flames created.

"Katrina, please." Sullivan was at her side, pulling her back. Her eyes met his and she melted in his arms. Sullivan had always been confident—but in this moment—he was scared. She no longer resisted his pull and let him drag her to the boat.

"Can you hold that wall until we're out of here?" he asked.

"Yes." She held her eyes on the blur of the white lab coat. A voice yelled from the other side of the wall and movement from all around caused the water wall to ripple. The remaining guards were trying to break their way through her protective barrier. She chuckled at their efforts. No one was getting past her magic.

She stepped inside the boat, and Sullivan pushed it offshore. Before he jumped aboard himself, he used his magic to make them and the boat vanish.

Katrina released her wall of water and it washed inland

over the mass of security guards, knocking every man down. Every man except Dr. Hunter. He remained standing, unaffected by her power. He walked to the water's edge and she swore he stared directly at her despite the invisibility Sullivan's power provided.

A grin washed over Dr. Hunter's face. That grin screamed victory. Connor was captured and Dr. Hunter still had Ebony and Charlotte. Even though she was escaping with Sullivan, that grin showed his confidence and told her he would one day control her power.

She would fight until her last breath and never give into him.

With a final flash of lightning, she called upon all the water of the river. Pulling it back, holding the water until the boat cleared the crest of the wave she created. With a single breath, she freed the wave. Crashing into the island's shore, the wave pushed them halfway across the river.

In a single breath, they were free, hidden with Sullivan's power of invisibility.

She fell to her knees and cried. All this time, Connor beat himself up for his mistakes, for failing at keeping his friends safe. But his failure was nothing compared to her own. Her blind trust in Ajax lead them into a trap.

Sullivan remained quiet and left her to cry while he rowed them the rest of the way across the river. When they reached the other side, she stood and wiped her face. She was done crying. Crying wouldn't get results and it was time to stand tall and be strong. She let herself be fooled by the first man to show her affection. A mistake she would never make again.

ACKNOWLEDGMENTS

Well! I did it again.

I was amazed I finished my first novel. I was even more amazed that so many of you loved it. I don't know why I always doubt myself, I guess it's in part our nature, but I'm glad I've stuck with this and have another novel out there in the world.

Richard, you support everything I do. No matter how crazy I think you'll think I am, you always stand beside me and never question my sanity (at least not outwardly). You understand my vision and more importantly, you want it for me just as much as I want it.

Victoria, Clarice, and Xavier—Everything I do, I do so you can have a better life than me. Your support, interest, and genuine love for what mommy does makes my life complete. Always ask questions and feed your imaginations. Your imagination will take you farther than any other skill or talent you possess.

Racquel Henry, my editor, friend, and colleague—I know I said this last time, but you will always be my favorite cheerleader. I love Writer's Atelier and will be forever grateful that the universe brought us together. Thank for being you and opening your heart to so many talented writers.

Here's to a lifetime of writing fascinating stories about far off places that only the imagination can take us.

Love,

DEAR READER

WOW – Thank you!!!

I am so super excited that you came back to continue this adventure with me! I hope you enjoyed the continuation of the Magical Bond Series. There's still so much story to tell and I'm grateful you're on this journey with me. It's a privilege that you chose my book among the thousands of choices available to readers. I hope to see you in the near future as the story continues in the next volume of this series, *Volume Three, In the Wake of Rebellion.*

If you loved the book, a favorable review would be appreciated. Reviews are an author's best friend and critical to our success. I've included the Amazon link to my book for your convenience so leaving a review will be easy. https://www.amazon.com/dp/B07DBJXKG2

If you didn't enjoy the book, I thank you for giving it a try. I would love to know what you didn't enjoy about my book. If you have feedback that could help me improve on my writing and storytelling, please email me at author@ambochnak.com.

Happy reading always.

A.M. BOCHNAK

Join my email list to stay up to date on upcoming new releases

Click here: http://eepurl.com/divWGb

Your next adventure awaits at www.ambochnak.com

AUTHOR BIOGRAPHY

A.M. Bochnak is an award-winning author for her debut novel *Fortitude Rising: Volume One of the Magical Bond Series*. She is a dreamer, always looking beyond reality for her next adventure. With her head in the clouds or her eyes turned to the stars, she spends countless hours imagining new adventures and far off worlds for which to travel. When she isn't dreaming, she writes science fiction and fantasy with her focus on epic fantasies, apocalyptic and dystopian fiction. *Fortitude Rising*, a sci-fi dystopian fantasy, is her first published novel. She is an American author, born and raised in southern Ohio and now lives in Gainesville, Florida.

CPSIA information can be obtained
at www.ICGtesting.com
Printed in the USA
BVHW031635260819
556809BV00008B/197/P